THE SHIP-WIL

A NOVEL OF VIKING WIRRAL

H.A. DOUGLAS

Copyright Roz White (writing as H.A. Douglas) 2008

The right of Roz White (writing as H.A. Douglas) to be recognised as the author of this work has been asserted by him in accordance with the Copyright, Designs and Patents Act 1988.
All rights reserved. No part of this publication may be reproduced, stored in or introduced into a retrieval system, or transmitted, in any form or by any means (electronic, mechanical, photocopying, recording or otherwise), without the prior written permission of the author. Any person who does any unauthorised act in relation to this publication may be liable to criminal prosecution and civil claims for damages.

This book is sold subject to the condition that it shall not, by way of trade or otherwise, be lent, resold, hired out or otherwise circulated without the author's prior consent in any form of binding or cover other than that in which it is published and without a similar condition including this condition being imposed on the subsequent purchaser.

This book is dedicated to my former wife Elvara and my
children Eleanor, Kendrick and Rowanne, who were a large part of its inspiration.

INTRODUCTION

This story is set on the Wirral peninsular, between the Mersey and the Dee rivers, in the year 919 AD. The political situation is as follows:
Sihtric Caech is the new Viking king of Dublin, having beaten off an assault by Niall Glundub, the Irish king of the northern Ui Neill, to secure his position. His kinsman Ragnar, having assisted in the re-establishment of a strong Norse presence in Ireland, has returned to Northumbria to be proclaimed King in York.
In what will soon become a united, single kingdom of England, Edward the Elder is consolidating his position as the new king of Mercia, following the death of his sister Aethelflaed "The Lady of the Mercians". Since the death of her husband Aethelred, she and Edward, the children of Alfred the Great of Wessex, have been systematically reconquering those parts of England surrendered to the Danish invaders by their father. English Mercia still follows the line of Offa's Dyke at this time, and so includes a large chunk of what is now North Wales. Beyond the Dyke is the Welsh kingdom of Powys, but this will be reduced in both size and influence by the emergence of Gwynedd.
The Wirral peninsula itself, although nominally Mercian, has since 902 been occupied by Norse-Irish refugees from a Dublin attacked and overrun by the Irish. Their numbers were such that within five years of arriving, they felt strong enough to claim Chester as well, and although this claim was comprehensively rebuffed by the Mercians - who refortified the city by way of answer - northern Wirral is effectively an independent Norse enclave, making its own laws and following its own, Norse, way of life. By the time of Aethelstan's accession to the Saxon throne in 925, however, Norse and Irish

moneyers will be an integral part of Chester's
economic miracle, making it the largest mint in the
country. But that is still to occur; for now, there is an
uneasy peace, while the Wirral's Norsemen look to what
Edward's plans are, and also watch the tangled skein
of events across the Irish Sea.
In "The Shipmaster", the previous volume in this saga, we followed the voyage of
Hrolf, son of Dubhnjall, and his companions in the
local *felag*, or ship-owning co-operative. But the
world does not sit idle whilst the men are gone; his
wife Var has her own problems closer to home, and it
is to those that we turn now...

AUTHORS NOTE

As with *The Shipmaster*, there is a strong personal component in this novel. A number of the main characters are drawn from people I know and love, and it is my hope that I have not upset or insulted anyone by any of the portrayals in this book. It was certainly not the intention.

I will also take this opportunity to apologise for the formatting. It has proved impossible with my limited knowledge and resources to modify the original, rather ancient files to improve the reading experience. I hope it does not detract too much from your enjoyment.

CHAPTER ONE

People stood and watched as a snake-like wooden ship, its prow and stern-posts sitting high and proud and its decking piled high with men and bundled belongings, rattled its oars back into the muddy waters alongside and slowly worked its way along the middle of a river, pulling away from them and their homes as if strangely reluctant to leave. Snatches of final farewells could be heard on the breeze between the slap of oars on water; on the shore, arms waved, throats yelled good wishes of their own, and eyes – some of them, at any rate – brimmed with unshed tears. Nobody moved from their places until the vessel was far away up the river, almost at its mouth and about to turn into the harsher currents of the wider, faster-flowing water to the north; then, on some intangible, unspoken signal, folk began to turn away, forming into smaller clumps, little knots of souls, ready for the steep climb back towards the hall and its houses that they all called home.

"Well then," sighed Var, wife to the ship's master and lady of the hall of Walea and Lisceardr, as she gathered her three children back to her and turned to her attendants, "here we are for another summer." Hild smiled reassuringly, her gentle face creasing only slightly at the edges of her mouth. "As you say, lady, just another summer, like so many others. Time to clean out all the corners, bring in fresh bedding, gather wood against the winter and keep the place running just as the lord would have it run... only we don't have his help to achieve it all!"

Var grinned. "It's alright for you: you don't miss his warmth and breath at the side of you every night, and you don't have the worry of whether he'll come back whole and hale – if he comes back at all. But you're right: the summer tasks are easier when he's gone, and as I said to him, I'd miss the wealth and the luxuries if he didn't sail every spring. It's just..." she waved her hands, trying to find the words. Hild nodded sympathetically; Ymma, so much younger, just looked wistful, and a trifle wary of the work still to come.

The path back to the hall was a steep one: it ran across the line of an escarpment that looked out over the marshes and river the ship had just left from. Beyond the marshy, flat ground lay the sea; if Var squinted into the haze of another spring day, she might just be able to see the little house of Kol and Arne, the newest recruits to her husband Hrolf's share of the crew. Together with Brynjolf, who lived to the east, Snorri, who dwelt to the far north, beyond even the wide bay of the big rivermouth, and Einar, who had just inherited his position in these parts from his uncle, Hrolf owned a share of a twenty-bench ship, and today was their leaving-day. They would not be back until the late autumn at the earliest; and as usual, there was any amount of unfinished business left in their wake. What with the death of Eyvind, Einar's uncle, so recently, everything was late in happening, too. The ship ought to have been away nearly a moon earlier, and so the crew would either have to cut their voyage short – and thus risk a smaller share of any booty – or take a gamble on staying out for the normal length of time and still being able to return as winter closed in across the sea. But although she worried about such things, they were not the main focus of Var's concern. The ship looked after itself; she just took her share of the profits when it came back, be that silver, cloth or any other useful thing. Her thoughts were more firmly fixed on matters closer to home.

She sent Kendrick, her son of seven or so years, and his younger sister Rowan, on ahead to see how far they could race each other before collapsing in the dirt of the track. As their shouts and laughter echoed away from her, she turned to Elle, her eldest.

"All this late leaving, and Eyvind's dying like that, means it's not so likely that we'll get to go visiting anywhere this summer after all. I'm really not sure that we'll have the time, or the manpower to spare."

"That's a shame," the girl replied. She was in her twelfth summer, Var thought, and had pulled on her best dress to see her father off on his travels. Her hair, bright gold in contrast to the darker shades of both her parents, was hidden behind a hastily-tied headscarf, although a lot of it still cascaded down her back towards her waist, and she had evidently raided her mother's jewel-box for beads to string across her front. Her face currently wore an aggrieved, pouting expression.

"I know; I was rather looking forward to it as well, remember," added Var. "But everything is all messed up right now, and your father might not even be back in time for the autumn Thing at this rate." She sighed, and for a few moments concentrated on just putting one foot in front of the other as they came to the steepest part of the climb. "All we can do for now is see how things go, and hope for some leeway later in the year. Do you know, I swear this hill's getting steeper!"

"Kendrick and Rowan don't seem to be having any trouble," retorted Elle with a smile that took some of the sting from her words. "It must be you getting older, mama."

"I notice you don't run off with your brother and sister though..."

"That's because I think I'm needed here instead – or maybe not!" she laughed as up ahead Kendrick took a tumble over a stray stone. Var watched as her daughter and her maidservant seemed to race each other towards the boy, who was already sitting up and rubbing his knee ruefully. The Lady of the Rock smiled to herself: it was time to shake off the winter and its attendant longing for hot fires, easy days, rich feasts and attentive husbands. Now came the summer, when she alone was in command.

CHAPTER TWO

The hall was warm and dark, warmer even than the promise of the day outside and without the harsh glare of the sunlight as it fought its way through the clouds. The fire had been made up with peat dug from the marshy ground at the bottom of the cliff, together with a little of their precious wood stock, and the tables were already being set up by the time Var walked through the door into the main room. Her people were already gathering for the day-meal; most of the faces were familiar, but scattered here and there were some new ones. Einar's men, she recalled suddenly, the extras he had brought in case she had need of them, and who couldn't be fitted into the ship. How many, she wondered: it would have a bearing on the amount of grain and meat they would go through between now and the harvest-time. Might she be better off sending them home?

She made her way to the High Seat without any of her concerns touching the soft contours of her face, and gracefully sat in her habitual place to one side of the carved and painted pillars in the middle of the hall. "So, then," she said as the noises of talking around her faded, "now is the time of the year when we make this place pay its way over the winter. There are fields to tend, animals to mind, mending to be done and tools to make and repair. Most of you know how it's done: you attend to your own work, and you only come to bother me if it's *really* a problem you can't find an answer to. There's enough of you in this place that somebody ought to be able to lend a hand or an eye or whatever else becomes needful: just as on the ship, we have to be a crew together, helping each other when needed and not making too many demands of those around us." For some reason, her gaze rested upon Thurbrand the cowherd and Yngvar the cookhouse-thrall as these last words came out. Var was well aware that there were problems brewing between them, and that it would most likely be up to her to sort them out.

"For today, though, we can ease into things," she continued smoothly. "As I say, most of you have your tasks and they're no different whether my husband, your lord, is home or not. You simply come and keep me informed, instead of telling him. You men who came over with your lord Einar: I will speak with you after the food and we'll sort out what to do with you for the best. Anlaf, are you in here?"

"Aye lady, I'm here." Anlaf half-rose, his thin face, bright eyes and ready smile clear to see. Var nodded. "Your master said to use you as headman over all the others, and so I shall, at least until we can get everyone sorted out and have a better idea as to how many are needed here." She settled herself back into her cushions and signalled for Hild to fill her cup.

"Well then," she said with a satisfied air as Yngvar reappeared with the first plate of bacon, "I think that will do for now."

CHAPTER THREE

"You keep a good and wealthy house, lady,"
smiled Anlaf as he came across the hall after the daymeal.
Var arched an eyebrow but returned the smile;
she found it unlikely that a man such as he was totally
unused to better living than the majority got. As she
waved him to a seat on the bench, they both watched
as men removed tables and stowed them back against
the low timber walls of the hall. Stools were taken
into corners; the iron pot over the fire was lowered
and fresh water added. There was very little in the
way of leftover food, but whatever there was would
find its way out to the chickens and the pigs soon
enough. The hall quietened; Hrolf's men went out to
attend to their daily tasks whilst Einar's withdrew
beyond the hearth and amused themselves with dice
and *tafl*.

"I find it hard to believe that your own lord hadn't
had something similar before he came to Wirhalh,"
Var began. "None of you look particularly starved,
and there are too many to suggest that you were all
living like bondar..."

Anlaf grinned again and brushed long, straight hair
from his eyes – although as it was cut low over his
face, it just flopped straight back again. "Ah, lady,
you have the mind of a ship-mistress! We were doing
well enough, but the lord Eyvind's message hinted
that we could have even more, and it was too good an
offer to refuse. A pity it had to come in the way it did,
though."

"From what I've heard, he knew his days were
numbered when his horse fell on him that day, and I
reckon he was more concerned about leaving
everything neat and tidy for those who came after him
than he was about his own well-being. He didn't send
messages to any of his ship-mates, for example; mind
you, there was probably little enough that could be

done, from what Hrolf said. All the same, I'd've been happier if Halldora had been given the chance to look at the wounds: she's a wonder in that regard."

"I can tell you that, no matter how great your woman's skill, and without wishing to contradict you at all, even the Gods would've been hard-pressed to mend the lord Eyvind's leg, lady," replied Anlaf. "It wasn't just broken: it was crushed. It didn't even look like a limb towards the end: just a mass of pulped meat hanging from the man." He shuddered. "I only got the one look, and I can still see it when I close my eyes. May the Gods preserve all of us from such a thing."

"I was hoping to visit later in the summer, but now I don't know: everything is late and out-of-sorts. On the other hand, once we have this place straightened and settled and can see how many extra hands I really need, it's likely that some of them could go home, and so I'd have an escort in one direction at least." She cleared a space between them by the simple expedient of throwing the debris to the back of the bench. "So tell me then: how many are here, what are their names, and what can they do for me?"

Anlaf looked thoughtful for a moment. "There's about a dozen or so left here now," he answered slowly, "all good men who can turn a hand to all sorts of things. My own lord kept his best people, those with proper crafts to follow, behind with my lady Thordis, as well as those of his best fighting-men who aren't on the ship – and all of lord Eyvind's men stayed on, of course."

"That's a lot for anyone to manage alone," murmured Var. "How is your lady at that game?" Anlaf grinned again. "Good enough, lady, but still finding her feet in this new place a bit. It's possible she is feeling the change in our luck more even than lord Einar is; one of the reasons for bringing so many men out with him was to give her a better chance at organising the place to her liking without having to worry about what so many men were going to be doing all at once. It will be easier to feed these others back in a few at a time, I'm told."

"You don't agree?"

"I have no idea, lady! I boss the men I'm given to run, but planning beyond that is not my concern – or not usually, at any rate. Part of me wonders how easy can it be, though, to have everything set up just right, and then get more hands coming in to maybe mess it all up again. Better, perhaps, to have everyone there from the start, and just shake them all until people fall into place. I don't know."

Var took a careful breath: the next question was one of the trickier ones. "Think she'd be happy about having another pair of eyes to come and look this soon after arriving?"

Again, Anlaf paused to consider. "I'd've said she would, aye, lady. She and Einar have not been married all that many years, and whilst I suppose they must be of a similar age to yourself and lord Hrolf, they've not begun the raising of children yet. She seemed glad enough of the help you sent to put lord Eyvind in his howe..."

Now it was Var's turn to pause and consider. "Then perhaps we might manage a visit this year after all," she murmured eventually.

CHAPTER FOUR

In the furthest recesses of the hall, lamps were clustered around the low platform that ran across one end of the *stofa*. Far beyond the brightness of the High Seat, and with the heat of the hearth still comfortable on their backs, Var and her ladies sat and contemplated the weaving that hung on the loom before them. For all that visitors were received closer to the fire, and Hrolf discharged his functions and obligations as *hauldr* from his own seat and its painted pillars, this was where the really important business, that of putting cloth on people's backs and on the yardarm of the ship, went on. Var's wool and linen were a vital part of the ship's cargo every spring, and their production came very high on the list of areas to allocate resources. Only the provision of their food came higher, as a rule. The roof-posts to either side were liberally dotted with iron lamp-stands, and Var had occasionally wondered about making an opening in the roof somehow, in order to let a little more light in. The loom itself was part of the houseframe: its vertical timbers were fixed firmly into the platform at their base and into the wall-plate at their top, with only a little space behind. Baskets of spare clay weights sat to one side, whilst bags of raw, unspun fleece left over from last summer hung from pegs in the roof-timbers. Somehow, amid the chaotic jumble of bags and baskets, Hild and Ymma found room to sleep here every night, too.

It was peaceful here – or at least, it usually was. This time, however, she eyed Yngvar balefully as he stood before her stool. The slave did his best to look innocent, and spread his hands wide.

"I'm sorry my lady, but the man was insistent on speaking with you. He waits at the hearth even now. I only brought the message, lady." Was there a hint of a sulk within his tone? Var couldn't decide, and eventually concluded that she didn't much care, either.

"And did he give a name?"

"He says he is Thorvald, lady, from the lord Snorri's holdings, and that he brings a message from his lady Gytha, for your ears."

Var frowned in thought. "What could Gytha be wanting that requires the cost of a messenger?" she wondered. Then she remembered. "Oh! Oh shit and damn!" she exclaimed. "I know what this is about," she went on, in answer to Yngvar's hurried step backwards. "Give him ale and tell him I'll be with him shortly. Tell him he can stay here for tonight, if he wants." She sighed and rose stiffly from her seat. "It's getting to be a busy summer this time around." She gazed longingly at the loom as she gathered up her cloak and wondered if there would be anything woven on it this year at all.

"Lady," Thorvald rose from his place at the bench and knelt as she flowed her way up the length of the hall. She signalled him to get up and be seated again as she took her own place between the pillars. Clearly this was going to be official business.

"I hear you are come from the lady Gytha," she said. "I think I probably know your errand, but give me the full message anyway, just so we begin from the same place."

Thorvald took another swallow and cleared his throat. "My lady Gytha sends her greetings to you, lady, and hopes that you are able to give a favourable answer. When your husband the ship-master came to announce his readiness to sail, there was discussion about his also sending an overseer to lend extra weight to my lady's words among her own thralls and the workers in the fields. My lady worries that they do not obey her as well as they ought, and the prospect of another summer without her own lord weighs heavily on her. Those are her words, lady, and she further asks if this offer of help is still open. If it is, she would accept it most willingly. That, lady, is the whole of the message, and I am to take your answer back with me, if I can."

"I knew of this," replied Var warily, "but what I *don't* know is what, if anything, my husband did about it before he sailed off for the summer. The man in question is one Solmund: a good man, a freeman and a former ship-man himself, although not on our boat. He went to Frankia, I believe, and then only last winter he married Linden, who had been one of my kitchen-house helpers for a while. They have a house down the slope a short way, and they're not used to the best of their talents, I'm sure. So I would imagine they would be happy to go with you to your lady, if only for the summer – but what do you think about it, Thorvald? Where in this do you stand?"

"I'm one of the lord Snorri's hearth-men, lady, but ships and I don't agree; besides, he fills his share of the crew readily enough that I've never needed to even think about going aboard. So I stay behind every year and lend a hand where I can. It's true enough what my lady says about the field-hands: they're an unruly lot, they don't live in the hall and so they feel they can do more-or-less as they please, within the bounds of actually getting the crops sown and harvested and the animals sorted, or none of us will eat come winter, them included. It's reached the stage where they need a new face, a strong arm, to whip them back into shape a little. They've got used to the idea that all the best men from the place go away every year, and there aren't enough left with the know-how to run the farms. I'm a fighting-man: I've never handled a hoe or a scythe in my life, and I wouldn't know a weed from an ear of wheat. Why should even the lowest of the thralls who breaks his back in those fields, listen to me?"

"I'm pretty certain that Solmund could tell the

difference between food and un-food," murmured Var thoughtfully. "We tend to put all our people into the fields at various times, whether it's what they do for a living or not. There aren't many exceptions: Jon the smith takes his turn if he's not too busy, although Grim tends to stay in his woodshed and make things..." She smiled as the thought faded away. "Solmund can be a hard-nosed bastard, of that there's no doubt: if he thinks he's right on an issue, there's often no budging him. I'd say he'd do well at bossing other, lesser men.

"The problem is, I've no idea how much – if anything – my husband said to him about it before he sailed away for the summer. They went over to Brynjolf's burgh together earlier this year, and then went straight on to Eyvind... but did they speak of it? I've no idea. They ought to have, they were together for long enough; but that doesn't necessarily make it so, does it?

"I think the best thing to do," she went on, "is to have you stop over for the night while I send a runner to bring Solmund and his wife up here to find out exactly what has been said. If he already knows about the idea, then we have an advantage, and just a few loose ends to tie up. If he doesn't... well, let's just say that it'll be my husband who'll have some explaining to do to your lady when he comes back in the autumn!"

CHAPTER FIVE

Solmund, like his new bride, was tall and lean, but where Linden's face had a warmth in its slightly softned features, Solmund had features seemingly carved from the stony bones of the earth. Bushy eyebrows, now turning grey, overhung a jagged nose that resembled a notched axeblade; wide cheekbones added emphasis to a narrow chin and a tight, thin mouth. But for all his craggy face, that mouth was frequently turned up at the corners in an easy smile, and there was humour and gentleness to be found in his dark grey eyes. He and Linden sat across the table from Var, who on hearing of their approach, had hastened back to the light and authority of the High Seat. Her weaving would have to wait yet again, although she didn't doubt that Hild and Ymma would do more in her absence. She also vaguely wondered where Yngvar was, and whether the oaf had done anything about the night-meal yet. They seemed to be collecting extra mouths to feed, and she had no intention of being thought stingy in the food.

"I am sorry to report, lady," Solmund drawled in his lazy, sardonic-sounding way, "that our lord said nothing to me about this idea of going up to the lord Snorri for the summer." He scratched the side of his nose idly and contemplated his cup for a few moments. "It's an interesting and attractive idea, but how far advanced it might be, I really couldn't say."

"Blast him!" grumbled Var. "There are times when I could wring my husband's neck – and they usually all come at once, within a moon of the boat leaving its shed and I discover all the things he's left half-done! Oh, curse it all: now I'll have to send messages to Gytha, and wait for her reply, and then try and get

something organised in time for any extra help to be of some actual use! We – your lord and I – were of the opinion that you might welcome the chance for a bit of advancement," Var went on more mildly, cautiously. "Certainly, Solmund, you've never made much secret of your opinion that you could do a lot more than you get to do here: that's been going on since long before he met you, Linden, believe me! So when this chance came up, well, naturally we thought of him – and thus, also of you."

"I appreciate your consideration, lady." Linden had a homely, usually welcoming face and a slight limp when she walked. Now that face was showing clear signs of worry and discomfort. "But we are newly wed, as you are well aware; we're still rather finding each other, so to speak. I do wonder if it's the best circumstance to head off into new places... we've not done anything to anger you or the lord Hrolf, have we?" There was anxiety in her tone suddenly; Var reached out a hand and patted the one now fidgeting in Linden's lap.

"No, there's nothing wrong, I promise. It's purely that Hrolf holds the opinion that your new husband is a capable man in a great many ways – ways that he'll not get much chance to show while you're living here. Gytha asked for help over the summer: she's getting old, and feeling it, and her bondar are starting to get lazy and awkward. She spoke the need for a strong, energetic headman to bring the others back into line, and Solmund certainly has the background for that, from what I've seen and heard. But it's not just about sending him where he'll do the most good: Gytha's not got much help in the hall, according to my own husband, and so your own skills would be of great value, too. This is a huge chance, Linden: you would go from here with our friendship and support, and perhaps even a handful of familiar faces to help get things under control. Your new husband will be in charge of the thralls and bondar around Snorri's lands – and his lands are pretty big – and you'll be running a house the size of this one, with women under you and only the lady Gytha to answer to! And I know you can do that," Var leaned closer with a smile. "You've taken charge of my own hearth from time to time when it's been needed, and you've fed us all splendidly. Between you, you're a strong power in any house, and it's that which Gytha needs right now, or there'll be nothing left by the time Snorri and the other men get home..."

Linden chewed a lip nervously. "It's a big step, lady, and one I'm not sure we ought to be taking. We're not lord and lady, after all: we're simple people, making our own living as best we can and trying not to upset anyone around us..."

"You're both free folk, not beholden to us beyond the payment of your rents and other dues," corrected Var. "Were you simple bondar, I could order you up the coast to Gytha, but once there, you'd not do any good – her people need someone superior in charge, 'cos from what I hear they have no respect for each other, or their current mistress. This really is a good chance to enchance your standing in the world even more; this is the first step towards a holding of your very own, with bondar of your own to run it. What you learn at Gytha's hall will stay with you - and there'll be rewards in it. Silver, gifts, the thanks of powerful men in that region... maybe even an offer to stay on and make a home there once the summer is over. We'd miss you both were that to happen, but I'm not about to stand in the way of a good wyrd snaking around you."

She turned her most pleading gaze on her visitors, quietly tapping the closest of the carved pillars. "Are you sure I couldn't ask this of you, Solmund? Would it not be possible to just begin this matter again as if Hrolf were still here and getting on with organising it as he ought to have done? Or must we send a message to our neighbour to say that we can't help her after all?"

Solmund held up a restraining hand. "My lady, nobody is talking about dismissing the idea! From what you have already said, I'm satisfied that the arrangement is a good one, and certainly to our advantage if we carry it off. It's just perhaps that it all came upon us rather... unexpectedly..."

"You're being more tolerant than I think I might have been," admitted their mistress, "but in truth, we have known you a good many years, Solmund, and I would like to think that we wouldn't just sell you off like some dim thrall, or put demands on you that only the lowest of bondsmen ought to put up with. You have your freedoms, and you have skills and abilities that aren't used to their fullest around here. We can't go uprooting all our own folk and their ways of doing things just to make better use of you – but the lady Gytha, from the sound of things, can. And would. And would be extremely happy to have two such capable people come in and take the burden of the farms from her."

"I know we make our own way in these parts," said Linden, "and that there isn't really anything much to hold us here... but it's home, all the same. Would it be too much to ask if we will still be welcome here when the summer is over and the lord Snorri is back home, however well – or not - this venture turns out?"

Var smiled warmly. "You would go with our support and friendship as I said just now, and you would be most welcome back here, should you choose to come. But my understanding is that there's a lot more land even to the north of Snorri's holdings, and not all of it taken. Good farmland, with rich, dark soils and plenty of timber for building, too. Or selling... should Snorri make you a decent offer to stay on, or should you choose to make a new home there regardless, you will always have the friendship of this hall. That I can promise you."

"You seem a lot happier to even think about it than I am right now," reflected Linden, as much to herself as to the man sat beside her. "It's all right for those whose lives have been a whole run of adventures, one after the other; but some of us have stayed at home instead. We've kept the house, run the farm or the trade, raised our bairns... all sorts of things, and all good reasons for staying put – at the time, at least."

"I didn't know you had children!" exclaimed Var suddenly. Linden smiled and arched an eyebrow. "That was long ago, lady: they're grown and gone out in the world."

"All the more reason to copy their example then, wouldn't you say?" suggested Solmund laconically. He shuffled closer to her side on the bench. "It's a summer: a summer to perhaps make our reputation and our fortune, lay the basis of a good, rich autumn together. As you said, my love, there's not really that much to hold us here, besides the friends we've made and the rents we owe. This gives a chance to make more friends, maybe take some of our current ones with us... and pile up the silver and our good names." He leaned back and stretched. "I'm for going, now that I understand why the request came from your quarter, lady, and not from the lord."

"Who simply ran out of time and gave himself too much to do," agreed Var. "So do you need a little while longer before giving an answer, or can I arrange to send her messenger back to Gytha that you're on your way?"

"Lady, let me have until tomorrow to finally be persuaded," requested Linden. "Leaving a place has never been an easy thing for me."

Var nodded. "That's fair enough. I'll also give you leave to go through the sheds and houses hereabouts and make a tally of anything you think you might want to take with you in the way of tools or weapons, that sort of thing. I'd also suggest that you go and have a word with Grim the treesmith and see about borrowing his wagon for the trip..."

"Lady," put in Linden once more, "would you think the lady Gytha will have a house for us on her lands, or would we be bedding in the hall?"

"I've really no idea: I haven't been over that way myself in some years. I'd imagine she has houses around her hall, just as we do here; it's hard to imagine Snorri letting the bondar into the hall, especially not with his hearth-troop there already. Should I tell the messenger to ask? It's no bother, and if you'd rather have a house put aside for you, it gives her a chance to have it ready." She leaned forward slightly, her face serious. "It's about three days on the road, as I understand it, since Hrolf sails it in one, as a rule; there's the river to cross, so we'll have to go and have a word with Ulfketil over at the birch-tree stands and arrange to borrow his boat – if it's big enough to take a wagon." She exhaled noisily and frowned. "Not such an easy thing, this, is it? Better to travel as light as can be, but it's not fair to expect you to head into something like this empty-handed and without your precious things." She ran a hand across a small box, made of timber but bound in iron, with a large, boxy lock on the hasp. "I have the key to this," she smiled. "I'll make sure there's enough going with you to more than cover your costs. And I'll have Grim carve us a token to say that you're among my best-regarded people, and go with my support and my
trust, just so Gytha knows the quality of folk she's getting."

"You are being more than generous, lady," replied Solmund, laying a hand on his wife's lap in reassurance. "I think you can count on our agreement to go."

Var nodded in satisfaction. "I'll get Thorvald in to take the message, then. Shall I say to expect you in, what... a se'en-night from now?"

Solmund nodded, stroking his beard. "Three days to travel and four to make ready... that would seem adequate, lady."

Var stretched out a hand. "So we have an agreement, then."

CHAPTER SIX

From the doorway of the hall, Var could hear the cattle calling to be milked. Around the ridge on which the hall actually stood, the homefield spread its green sward across the gentle slope to the east; at its farthest end stood a cluster of smaller houses, faintly reminiscent she was often told, of the buildings within the timbered walls of her people's *longphorts* along the coasts of Ireland. She had never seen them, but Hrolf had – quite apart from his own sailing trips, his father had been one of Ingimund's men, one of those who had made it out of Ath Cliath when the native kings had risen against them and driven the northmen out. Var was from Mann, where houses were made from sensible materials such as stone and turf and good, solid wood; try as she might she could not see any purpose in making a house from woven hazel and very little else. The wind would be unbearable, surely, and as for the rain...

She sat on one of her special ornately-carved benches, just outside the hall's porch but still within the overhang of the roof, watching the day as it slid gently into twilight. To the west, across the low ground and beyond their little river, the ocean's waves pushed into the shallowly-sloping sand, and as she watched them her thoughts inevitably wandered out towards her husband and his crew. They were somewhere on those same waves, she knew; she seemed to remember him saying something about heading for Ongle-sey and then perhaps southwards towards one of the coastal phorts whose houses had begun this whole train of thought. From her seat high above them, the waves did not look too dangerous; she hoped it was the same wherever Hrolf and his shipmates were. It was nearly a fortnight since they had set off: realistically, they could be anywhere by now, although the Frankish lands might still be a little beyond them. She sighed and shrugged the thoughts away; from within the hall, she could hear the voices of her children and they were loud enough to nearly be competing with the increasingly anxious calls of the cows.

Then she heard another sound. Whereas she might have been content to sit and let her housemaids deal with whatever the youngsters were getting up to, and whereas she would have sat all night if need be and waited for Thurbrand to milk the cows as he was expected to, this was a noise that had her rising gracefully from her seat as soon as she heard it. The sound of a horn, not so distant. That meant visitors; which meant preparations and a welcome to be arranged. She brushed a little dirt from her dress and ducked back inside the door.

"Did anyone else hear that?" she called stridently from the passageway. Sounds of activity within the main room lessened, then stopped altogether. Var frowned.

"That's not an invitation to stop and listen: it's a simple question!" she barked. "Did anyone in there hear the horn being blown?"

"I haven't blown the horn, mama," came Kendrick's voice almost instantly. His mother smiled despite herself.

"I didn't ask if anyone had been blowing *our* horn," she replied. "I just heard another one, from out beyond the homefield. So start clearing this place up a bit: Hild, Ymma, how far off is the night-meal? When did the meat go in?"

"I'll haul the kettle down, mistress," said Yngvar hurriedly. The big, blackened pot duly thumped into the middle of the hearth, sending showers of tiny sparks in all directions. Var cursed silently, but held her tongue whilst the women prodded lumps of... sheep?... with a knife. There appeared to be some dispute about whether it was properly done or not; faces turned in her direction, seeking guidance and reassurance.

"I do not for a moment believe that you people are incapable of stewing something as basic as sheep!" Var fumed – but she went closer and drew her own knife with which to examine the morsels. "Still a way off," she decided quickly, "look and see how it doesn't run quite clear from the cut yet. Put it back in, but add the carrots and the cabbage, and maybe a jug of the master's ale, too. You have my permission for that. We might need to put some barley on as well." While Hild and Ymma went about their tasks, Var turned her attention to the rest of the hall.

"Everybody's outside still," she murmured, "and those tasks won't wait, either." She turned back towards the hearth. "Once that is attended to, we need to straighten up the benches and sweep through here. That includes you three," she said more sternly as her offspring tried to sneak out of the doorway. "Start bundling things away and spreading out the rugs for me. I'll go for the broom."

"Who is it that's coming?" asked Ymma. Var raised an eyebrow expressively.

"Now how am I supposed to know that, child? Have they sent a messenger? Are my eyes so strong that I can make out folk's faces clear across the hill? I wish they were, it'd make easier work of that tapestry! But I don't know; but that shouldn't stop us being ready to welcome even the sons of Ingimund themselves – although I can't imagine what would bring them all this way. So we will want bowls of water for washing, and as many clean cups and plates as we can find..."

"Will you be wanting your better dress out, lady?"

"Yes, indeed I will – but not until I've finished with the broom!"

CHAPTER SEVEN

By the time runners were coming in from the outfield, that patchwork of rough grazing and cultivated strips of land that stretched in one direction almost into the scattered homesteads known collectively as Walea and in the other out into the marshes and dunes that led to Meols, the hall was ready to receive its visitors. The long wall-benches were clear of personal belongings and other detrius, fresh fat had been smeared into the little wall-lamps and the plain, hardened earth floor had been properly swept. Sheepskins and woven rugs covered the tops of the benches, and the cleanest of the tables had been swiftly set up on their trestles. The one in front of the High Seat even had a cloth over it; in the fire, extra pottage had been hurriedly put on to cook, and more bread set to rise under an upturned pot.
"Well, that's about as good as it gets," decided Var as she looked around. "You two go get something clean on, if you have it, then do the same for the bairns." She turned her gaze from her handmaids to her eldest child. "Elle dear, you can sort yourself out, I'm sure. Go do it now, and then lend a hand to the others, alright?"
"Won't you need some help, mama?"
"Very probably but I'll call when I do, I promise."
Var glided past the fire towards the bed-closet that was built into the corner of the hall. The chest she shared with her husband sat just outside it, taking up its own share of the bench-space, but also ensuring that none of those who slept in the hall could ever bump against the walls of her own bed. One of the women – probably Hild, she thought from the look of things – had excavated her very best dress from the chest and laid it out inside the bed: a bright but pale pink linen shift with pleats all over it that were close to impossible to put back in after it had been worn,

and a woollen mid-green top-dress, that shade of green that could only ever come from putting the weld plants to boil in an iron pot. Like the linen, then, difficult to achieve without considerable expense and effort: just the sort of thing to impress guests with. She undid the clasps on her brooches and laid them, with their attendant strings of beads and trinkets, carefully on the bed before pulling off her everyday yellow dress and plainer shift. Her husband's lands might technically fall within the boundaries of the Mercians but she had never seen any reason, or felt any desire, to adopt the Englisc style of a single garment with sleeves and no place for adornments. The brooches, fist-sized shells of gilded bronze, had been her grandmama's back in the North Way, before her family had even gone to Mann. She liked the continuity, the flow, within the idea; it seemed to echo in the fullness and the flow of her dress as it swirled around her. Getting the top layer on was more of a struggle, and it was at this stage that she was likely to need the assistance of Hild or Ymma. But for once, she managed. Evidently the Gods were with her today: so who could their visitor be?

"What news?" she asked the earliest messengers as she gained the High Seat and settled herself in Hrolf's traditional place.

"Horsemen, lady, coming from the east – but probably from along the southerly road. Well appointed, from what we could see: there was the glint of iron among them..." replied Bjorn breathlessly. He pulled his comb and the length of braid that came with it from around his belt and attempted to straighten his windblown hair with it.

"Well, it's not so likely that horses would come from ocean to the west, now is it?" Var replied a little caustically. "But what makes you say that they came on the southern road? That would take them past Oslac's steading, and Thorstein's *tun*... we don't know so many folk along that road," she mused quietly. "I'd not be expecting visitors from that direction – or expecting them even less than I might from the northern shore, at any rate."

"Lady, they appeared among the sand-dunes, coming from the direction of the mounds around Meols. That's what made us think they took the southerly road," said the older of the two.

"Hmm: that's a strong argument, I grant you. Very well, Wulfstan, get a cup of something from Yngvar out in the kitchen before you go – but I'll need you and your lad's eyes back on them before very long, y'hear? I'll set others to watching as they come closer: I can't imagine where else such a fine company would be going in these parts. They must be coming here..." she tapped her cup on the edge of the seat in frustration. "I want to know who they are!"

As Wulfstan and his son departed, she turned to Ymma. "Go and find Anlaf: ask him in my name to get a few of his lads together and hold 'em around the hall. I don't think they'll need weapons – well, maybe give one or two of them the wood-axes and some of the spears – but I'd like a few men close by until we find out what's going on. I'm assuming these travellers are friends: they're blowing their horns and not trying to hide from us, after all; but there's still time for things to change. You understand?"

Ymma bobbed a curtsey with a trace of worry in her eyes. "Aye, lady."

"And ask Yngvar to come and tell me how it goes in the cookhouse!" Var called to her retreating back. She sat back in the High Seat and surveyed the hall once again. "And now we wait," she muttered impatiently, "and now we wait."

CHAPTER EIGHT

There could be no doubt that the meat was well and truly done by the time Anlaf sent his companion Egil back towards the hall with some proper details of who their visitors actually were. The man came into the gloom of the house, squinting slightly at the sudden absence of light and vainly trying to wave the smoke away from his eyes. None of those he met on his journey saw fit to delay him, or even see to his comfort before he had delivered his news. Var had not moved from her position in the High Seat, but she watched his approach in the same way that a hawk might watch a vole or a hare far below.

"Lady," Egil began, "my master's headman Anlaf bade me come with information. The man who comes riding is one Onund: he says he farms at Hrafnkelsby, and that your own lord would know of him..."

"I've heard his name," agreed Var, "but that's all I've heard. Hrafnkelsby's a bit out of our usual routes for travelling; doesn't it border on your own lords' lands? I'm sure it does... who would know for sure, I wonder, that isn't away on a ship? More importantly, why is he coming at this time? I thought everyone in these parts knew when the ship-going season was; or maybe he's too far away to have realised." She cupped her chin in one hand thoughtfully. "I wonder what he wants? Never mind: I daresay we'll find out soon enough. Go back to Anlaf, man, and ask him to do this Onund the honour of escorting him in. Somehow, I doubt I could rake up a decent enough showing from my own folk: all the best are away, of course. If we're going to start getting guests at all times of the year, I might have to do something about that."

She waved Egil away, and went back to wondering what someone like Onund, someone with whom she could not recall ever having had any business, and from the farthest ends of Ingimund's lands, could possibly want at Lisceardr.

The sound of horns, once so distant, gained rapidly in note for a short while before stopping altogether as the incoming riders met those men sent out to greet them. "Go outside," she said quietly to her younger two children, "and watch for these men. Once you have had a good look at them, come back in and tell me how they look, what sort of things they are wearing, how much armour they carry. Think you can do that?" Kendrick gave her a withering look and took his little sister's hand in order to lead her outside. "Can I go too?" asked Elle from the shadows behind the High Seat. "Or is there a reason why you singled those two out?"

"Partly because I hadn't realised you were there," her mother replied, "but also because you're of an age to be sitting in here and learning more important lessons, such as how to receive visitors of quality, as these folk appear to be. It's not in any way the same as hearing what the bondar have to say: there are rules about how things ought to be done, and it's high time you were learning them. If I consider you old enough to be fishing for offers of bethrothals, as I did at the Thing, then you're also old enough to be learning the ways of the household, eh?"

Elle nodded, although there was a look of disappointment on her face. "Don't scowl," reprimanded Var gently, "there'll still be other days for running around outside. But for this day, I want and need you in here." The indignant snort that came as reply suggested that her daughter was far from convinced.

There was suddenly an influx of people; the level of noises outside the hall rose again, with voices, stomping hooves and the snorts of good, strong ponies, their harness jingling with bells and other decorations. Var heard voices she did not recognise;

subconsciously, a hand went out towards Elle, both to reassure the girl and comfort the woman. "Should we stand?" whispered Elle urgently.

"No, or at least not yet," replied Var. But her eyes remained fixed on the door that led to the passageway, through which bright daylight was shining.

"My lady," called Anlaf, striding into the hall ahead of a knot of men who still wore their riding cloaks over what looked like much better clothing. "Onund, master of Hrafnkelsby, requests your guesting and hospitality. Should I admit him?"

"Now we stand," hissed Var, matching action to words. "Be welcome, Onund," she said to the strangers, in a ringing tone that held none of her worry or curiosity – yet. "Be welcome: come and sit, without weapons, and as friends. We will guest you gladly, and hear all you have to say."

She imperceptibly waved Hild and Ymma forward, with a soapstone bowl of clean, freshly-drawn water and Hrolf's largest horn, filled to the brim with ale. The man whom she assumed was Onund pulled off his hooded cloak – made from good, thick wool, she noticed – and beamed a smile.

"My thanks to you, my lady; I am Onund, Aethulwulf's son." He splashed water on his face as custom demanded and then took up the horn. "May good fortune smile on such a gracious host as you."

"Master Onund – or do I belittle you with such a title? I'm afraid I know nothing of you, sir, but I mean no insult. But you are truly welcome here, although, with such a slight acquaintance between us, I can't imagine what has brought you so far from home, either." She smiled in an effort to soften her words. Onund merely smiled again, and took the seat beside her own that she indicated. His men, once also divested of riding-clothes, ranged themselves around the hearth. Var noticed that Anlaf and his own lads did likewise.

"My business is simple, lady. I saw you at the Thing, when Einar Ivarsson got his rights in regard to Eyvind's old place, and I overheard that you were looking for matches for your lovely lass here." He grinned across at Elle, who suddenly shrank back into the shadows; Onund raised an eyebrow, but returned his attention to the lady of the house.

"I didn't get a chance to introduce myself, one way and another, but I thought such a chance just too good to miss. And so, my lady, I am here to make a marriage offer to your daughter."

CHAPTER NINE

The hall was quiet. The fire had been banked in the hearth, leaving only the faintest of dull-red glows showing through its ashes and embers; the mutton-fat lamps had all but burned out, and now just sent tiny beads of light to wash the wall-timbers around them. Along the walls, wrapped under blankets and cloaks, Lisceardr's own folk and its visitors slumbered, shadowy mounds huddled on benches, making a little landscape all of their own. But the lady of the house still sat in her husband's seat, her face thoughtful and her eyes troubled. Around her, lit only by dull lamplight and the restless, buried heart of the fire, other faces showed as patches of light and darkness.

"Well, this is a pretty situation," Var murmured eventually. "Of all the things that might have happened this summer, I hadn't been expecting this one."

"Quite something for a man such as Onund appears to be to leave his own hearth and travel so far in pursuit of a bride," agreed Anlaf.

Var smiled wryly. "It was me that suggested parading her around the Thing-site... so why am I so surprised that somebody actually noticed, and has risen to the hook? She's a good catch, of that there's no doubt: she can spin and cook already, and shows every sign of being a decent weaver and mender. I don't doubt that she'll be a credit to any hall she enters. And yet..."

"Yes, lady?" prompted Hild gently, her own face a mirror for Var's own, as yet unspoken, concerns.

"There's something I can't put a finger on: something not quite right. Onund's not anywhere near his grave yet, but he's... I don't know... older?... than I'd perhaps expected her matches to be. And probably older than *she* was expecting, too; I wonder what the chances of getting bairns by him is likely to be? And why isn't he married already?"

"Lady, these are all questions that can be answered in time," advised Anlaf, his angular face showing all its lines and hollows in the strange, diminished light. "Master Onund has only just arrived here; it has hardly been polite to question him too closely so soon. But tomorrow is another day, and there ought to be time enough for finding out what you need to know of him."

"He's a neighbour of yours," recalled Var. "While I know you've not been long in these parts, have you or your own lord had any word of him?"

"Only what the Lawspeaker told my lord Einar at the Thing, and that was little enough. Onund was, he said, unhappy that my lord's uncle, Eyvind, arranged his legacy so well that there was no chance of grabbing a little of what was there. But it's only one man's word on that, for all that his words ought to carry some weight. I'm not aware of any actual moves on Onund's part, and I'm pretty sure my lord would have told me."

Var nodded in understanding. "You've been together for some years, as I understand it?"

"Since we were lads, lady. I was one of those who went out and put his initial proposals to Hrafn, father of my lady Thordis."

"Never sought a bride for yourself?"

"Once," Anlaf's eyes clouded momentarily. "But that was long ago, and it didn't work out."

"Well, this is a new place, with new chances," replied Var gently, sensing a change in his mood. She smiled thoughtfully. "Maybe Onund sees things the same way." She stretched and put down her cup. "As you say, there is time for questions tomorrow. Quite how we're going to keep him entertained for another two days is an interesting question in its own right. I can only take his proposal so far without Hrolf and Oslac here to make the bargain; but he's a man of property and wealth, so he must know this already, surely. So why come and make the offer to me?" Her chin sank back down onto her gently-closed fist as she pondered the problem. "Why to me? Why now, when there was time before the ship set out – not that he'd have had that particular bit of information, of course, or not directly at any rate..." Her eyes focused again on the concerned faces studying her own in the lamplight. "What?" she demanded.

"Lady," smiled Hild, "you're thinking yourself into circles and knots! Your cup is empty; the fire is banked, and the porridge-pot is in the embers. There's nothing to be gained by sitting up all night chasing answers that can more easily be got come morning."

"So you're suggesting I go to bed, and let you do the same?"

"If it please you, lady, aye."

Var carefully undid her brooches and gathered both of them, and their attached strings of beads, into her cupped hands. "It's a fine thing when the servants are running the house instead of the mistress," she grumbled good-naturedly. "You just wait until morning: it'll all be back how it ought to be, you wait and see."

Hild chuckled. "Lady, if I can go back to our weaving and the minding of the fireside, I'll be happy."

CHAPTER TEN

"You must be aware, sir," Var began once the daymeal was out of the way and those not with immediate tasks to do had settled into distant parts of the hall for games of *tafl* or other recreations, "that much as I'm happy at your interest in Elle, I can't agree to anything definite without my husband here, or the Lawspeaker, come to that." She leaned back a little and rested her eyes on Onund appraisingly. "I did wonder what brought you here at this time of the year, when the ship is out and there's not much business can be concluded – or even advanced, really, I suppose."
Her visitor looked surprised. "Surely, lady, you hold the keys here? Mothir often said that whoever had the keys to the household chests could do anything; and I certainly recall her dealing with any amount of things that cropped up whenever *my* father was away."
"True enough, but we're not discussing the buying or selling of a few cows here, are we? You're right enough in that I run the hall and the farm-work, even when Hrolf *is* at home: that's my part of our marriage bargain, as it sounds your own mother did. But betrothals come under the heading of contracts and then we get into the realms of legality... you would want such an undertaking properly witnessed, would you not, and all above-board and legal? I'm pretty certain I do, and I daresay even Elle herself would want a say in that as well!" She paused for a swallow of ale. "No, sir, I'm afraid we will have to wait upon Hrolf and the other ship-men before we can do anything formal and binding: it is his authority that holds the law in these parts, and he that has the obligation to oversee pretty much any sort of dealing between households. But he ought to be home well before the winter really sets in; is there a problem with waiting?"

"Oh no: not at all," Onund smiled. It was a winning sort of smile, Var had to admit: not too broad or in danger of becoming a leer or a grin. Just a slight upturn of the mouth at either side which, coupled to a pair of striking blue eyes and a wavy mass of pale, almost white, hair, made this man of her own age or more still very attractive.

"I was eager to come as soon after the Thing as I could manage," Onund continued. His voice was smooth and rich, with none of the crackly quality that came from too much time either indoors with the peat-smoke, or too many days in an open ship, breathing in spray and shouting just to be heard. "I did not want to find myself at the wrong end of a long line of potential husbands; I am aware that I am, perhaps, a little older than might be expected for such a bride, and I was anxious to be heard along with any other, younger men who took a fancy to the lass. But I am healthy and whole still, with a good land-holding at Hrafnkelsby and good connections among the Mercians still."

"Still?" enquired Var.

Onund nodded. "My father's family are from Mercian stock: there is a rumour that mothir's might even have come out of Wessex once upon a time, although that link has proved hard to confirm."

"So you – or your family on your fathir's side – have lands within Mercia, as well as at Hrafnkelsby?"

"There is a holding out towards Wherington, but I've not been that way in many years: not since my father died, in fact." He waved a hand dismissively. "It's not my branch of the family, so I don't consider it as important to me as my own holdings."

"I was merely thinking in terms of setting the brideprice," Var explained. "For her part, Elle would come with a substantial dowry: a share of the lands here are set aside for her, and there might be the chance of a share in the ship's profits – although that would have to be taken from our own share, of course. But it could also be increased were you to come in as a Felag-man yourself, and buy a share of the ship..."

Onund shook his head. "I don't think that's so likely to happen, lady. I'm not a sailing man."

"No matter; and as I say, a share of whatever the ship has made in terms of cargo or profit is likely to be put into the deal anyway. Whatever agreement we eventually come to, I'm sure you'll find Elle's contribution to the marriage acceptable, if not even generous," smiled Var once more, and the talk turned to other matters.

CHAPTER ELEVEN

Spring advanced slowly into summer, imperceptibly; as the days lengthened, the sun grew warmer on the backs of the men in the fields, and the insect life around the midden seemed to increase tenfold. There was less frost on the ground when people first poked their noses out of doors, and across the ocean, the glitter of the waves seemed to stretch ever-further. But to Var, one of the surest signs that the world was running at its proper pace was the everthickening roll of cloth wrapped around the top of the loom. This particular length was a diamond-patterned twill in three shades of reddish-purple, and although it had yet to be cut off and examined properly in the daylight, it showed every sign of being a shimmering, smooth fabric that would fetch the highest of prices.

"I'm almost tempted to take this one into Legacaester myself and see what we can get for it," exclaimed Var as she and her companions sat around the end of the hall. "We're nearly out of the wool set aside for it, aren't we? What do we fancy doing next?"

"Were it likely to be listened to, I'd vote for a day away from the loom before we start re-warping it," commented Hild darkly. "That's the hurtful bit, the part I really detest. Could we not do a little more on the tapestries before we start off again? It'll take us the best part of a few days just to tie all the threads to their weights, and then we have to loop the right ones to their heddles... I get a headache every time we have to do it." She smiled with a sigh. "If I had the wealth, I'd have a thrall all of my own, whose only job would be to re-warp my loom for me and not complain about it."

"I'm not sure I'd want to trust any of ours with such a delicate and important task – certainly not Yngvar," Var chuckled. "Can you imagine his fat fingers on our lovely threads? No thankyou!"

"Given how little we see of him in here outside of mealtimes, I don't think there's much danger of having him volunteering for the job," Ymma reassured her. "Perhaps after this tricky one we could do something a little easier? Less demanding on the brain?"

"And of less value in whatever market it ends up in?" retorted her mistress. "No dear, we can't have that: it's only the complexity and cleverness of our cloth that makes it stand out from all the rest. Admittedly, we've yet to see anything from Thordis, her being so new to the district and so forth, but nobody else in these parts has been able to match us in the quality of our wool for some time. Before Gytha started losing the use of her fingers as they swelled, she turned out some of the best cloth I've ever seen: up to five heddles in her prime, I'm told. I'd love to get my hands on some of that... but practically everyone can produce basic stuff, Ymma. There's no pride in that, or value either, beyond the money saved by not having to buy it in. So no, we can't do something simple. What we can do is have a day outside when the sun shines, and go through the dyed stuff we already have, see what it *really* looks like." She looked around at the baskets of raw, plucked wool, and the skeins of spun thread that hung from the roof-beams like heavy woollen cobwebs. "And from the look of things, I'd say it was time to go and tell Yngvar we'll be wanting a fire under the dyepot again. There's an awful lot there waiting to be coloured, and precious little already done."

"That, lady," said Hild dolefully, "is because we've already used it all!"

CHAPTER TWELVE

Thurbrand the cowherd was sitting on his little bench, the one he kept by the fence of woven birch saplings that ran from the cowshed along the line of the ridge. Its closeness to the hall doorway meant that he invariably saw everything and everyone that went on around the big house, which tended to quietly annoy his master, who considered that the primary business of a cowherd ought to be the care and management of the cows. Conversely, Var felt that an extra pair of eyes outside was no bad thing, provided the cows didn't suffer from such neglect. Like her husband, she found that her time was too short, and had too many demands put upon it, to allow her to keep abreast of everything that went on around her extended household. Thurbrand's observations occasionally helped.

Today, however, he showed no inclination to be communicative. He watched stoically as Hild and Ymma panted and gasped and heaved the hall's huge baskets of processed wools out into the daylight. He did eventually rise to his feet once Var had also appeared, but his demeanour was one of reluctance even then. She twitched a frown on meeting his eye, and then decided to studiously ignore the old man. It took very little to get him crotchety, and whatever the cause on this occasion, it was unlikely to be of immediate or direct interest to her. Had Thurbrand thought otherwise, he would have made his own way into the hall already.

"Busy days, lady," Thurbrand eventually said by way of greeting, having slowly edged closer to the women and their work. Var looked up from the skeins of wool now draped over the fence and raised an eyebrow.

"Aye, that they are; but evidently not for our cows, eh?" She smiled as she said it, to take any sting out of the words. Thurbrand was a bondsman, part of the household and paid for his services, and he had his pride because of it. She couldn't make him the butt of a joke in the way Yngvar often was – at least, not within his hearing. "I believe Anlaf has taken our guest out into the dunes, hunting," she went on. "I'm not sure what he intends to catch, but since their homesteads run alongside each other it's probably more than just a bit of extra food he's chasing."

"Oh, there's plenty to catch if you set your snares right," replied Thurbrand cryptically. "But as you say, lady, I'd reckon there's more to the trip than just the chance of a hare or two."

"Who is it has sheep down there sometimes?"

"Ah: that'll be one of Vigdis' neighbours, out on the other side somewhere. Nobody bothers with fences out that way: it's wild ground, rough and hard going, so unless they've got a mark on 'em, you might never find out whose they are."

"If they're not marked, I might send a lad or two to go and put *our* mark on them! I bet we'd find out soon enough whose they are then." She turned back to the wools. "D'you think there'd be enough to make a shirt out of that reddish one?"

"Hard to tell until we weave it, lady," said Ymma.

"Maybe if we put another hue as the warp, though," murmured Hild. "We've got some blue from the heathers, those ones we gathered last year, or there's yellow..."

"Well, lady, if you're thinking of making more colours, you might want to be certain of your firewood," growled the bondi. Var smiled to Hild and Ymma, and winked.

"Aye? I heard you'd spoken with my husband about something similar, but that was before he sailed, of course. Got any further with your suspicions, then?"

Thurbrand nodded knowingly. "I've set a few snares of my own, lady. I'm just waiting to see who falls into them, now."

"I take it these traps are not the type to deprive me of any manpower at a time when I might need it most?"

"Not at all, lady. I'll come to you before I actually take things any further: you have my word on it."

"I've allowed Yngvar to practice at brewing; and I'm keeping an eye on the fires in the kitchen as well – and he knows I'm watching," added Var. "So that's fine, then, isn't it; I'm assuming that it's still Yngvar who's the subject of your suspicions?"

The cowherd nodded, his eyes dark and hooded.

"Well, I don't want *anything* done about it whilst Onund is here," she concluded firmly. "Come to that, I'd rather you didn't take matters any further even whilst Anlaf and his house-mates are staying with us, too. So I'd brace yourself for a long, patient summer if I were you, Thurbrand. And try not to let it get in the way of your proper work, hmm? Now if you've nothing to go and do right away, you can lend a hand back into the hall with this lot. We'll warp up the yellow, and make a weft of the red. If Hrolf doesn't like the colour for himself, we can get good silver for it in Legacaester come the winter, I'm sure."

CHAPTER THIRTEEN

Later that day, togther with Hild, Ymma and the children, Var walked the short distance along the ridge on which her hall sat. The day was still dry, if now turning a little overcast: the hills of the welsh lands to the south were unlikely to be visible on a day like this, and she was reminded that her husband often used that view as an indicator of the weather to come. The ground underfoot was sticky, but not actually wet; she made a mental note to go and see Thurbrand or someone about putting some straw down for a day or two – if they had any to spare, of course. It was still early in the season, and this year's crop had not been harvested yet.

As the ridge sloped gently downwards towards the shingle and waves of the ocean's edge, she passed the clustered homes of many of her bondsmen. Their little houses were mostly just hazel or birch wattle, with a splash of muddy daub to try and hold out the wind that had a tendency to blow in from the sea, and bring its salty, cold spray with it. Thatch never lasted very long in these parts; flimsy though the buildings undoubtedly were, most of them still sported heavy roofs of thick, green turf, and they relied on huddling together behind more panels of wattle to keep out the worst of the climate. Every once in a while one would collapse under the strain, and it was always, somehow, up to Hrolf as *hauldr* to fund the rebuilding – in exactly the same place, and in exactly the same style, with exactly the same underlying flaws. But nobody seemed to mind.

"Look!" said Kendrick excitedly, his arm dramatically pointing ahead of them. "There's Grim and his wagon!"

"Then that'll be where Solmund and Linden have been living," replied his elder sister with the infinite patience of her twelve summers. She sniffed. "I can't say I'm surprised at their wanting to move somewhere better."

"This is good housing for a lot of people," chided her mother gently, "and no being rude about it in front of them, even if they are only the bondar to the hall. An insult is a bad thing in anyone's life, and frequently needs repaying before it can be rubbed out."

"I bet fathir would deal harshly with anyone who tried that," Elle countered.

"Well he's not here to do it, is he? Besides, we didn't come here looking for arguments and battles. We came to see Solmund and Linden away safely, and send them off with good wishes and our friendship, remember?"

The freeman and his wife had a slightly larger house, although once inside it was still only the one big room. Its roof-posts were still sturdy, showing no signs of the rot that attacked so many of them as they rested, year after year, in mud that somehow never quite dried out at the bottom of the holes in which they stood. The walls had been recently patched with fresh daub – it had not quite dried to the usual offwhite colour, and there was the faintest whiff of the cow-dung that had gone into its making. Linden turned at the sounds of their entrance, her hands full of pale pink woollen fabric.

"I think my mother intended it to become a new dress," she said ruefully, "but it never made it off the walls. Still, as a gift it was a good one, especially from her, and at my time of life." She folded it deftly and placed in among a growing stack of items on the end of the raised wall-bench. "Lady, I'd offer a seat, but the only stools we have are in the cart already..."

Var gave a faint smile. "And the fire's nearly out, too: we came just in time, it seems."

Linden laughed. "Too soon to fix the new rent but too late to drink the farewell cup! Not to worry, my lady: it was good of you to come anyway. We're nearly done: Solmund's away returning a few borrowed things and making a few gifts to folks we think worth it. Had you heard that Asbrand and his family are going to follow us over to lady Gytha? If you permit it, of course," she added hurriedly.

"Aye, they came to see us about it, and they go with our agreement," Var assured her. "I'm going to ask Anlaf to send a couple of Einar's lads with you as well, although they're only going to act as your escort on the road. Any other time, I would have come with you and made the introductions properly: but we've got Onund here, and all these folk from Einar's hall as well... once you're safely with Gytha those men must come back again: they aren't mine to send away, after all, and the only place they ought to be going is back to their own homes. And if anyone else useful asks to follow, they're likely to get a favourable answer – providing there aren't too many, of course."

Linden bobbed a curtsey. "You are very kind, my lady, and we won't forget your generosity. Would you object if I carried on loading? Otherwise, the job just gets longer..."

"I know that feeling," smiled Var. "But I don't think you'll make it on to the road today. When the work's done, come to the hall for the night-meal: we'll find you places on the benches for the night, and you can head out early in the morning. By that time I can have Anlaf organised as well, you see, and their horses saddled. Far better to get an early start and a full day's travel than have to stop again almost before you get anywhere."

"I can put that to my husband, but I'm sure he can be persuaded."

"Splendid! We'll leave you to it, then: come along, bairns, out of the way now. Time to head back home again: we have a feast to prepare!"

"Will I get a feast if I go and stay with my uncle

Ragnar?" asked Kendrick as they slipped and stepped their way back up the slope.

"Of course," Var reassured him, "and this won't be a proper feast anyway: I said that just to give it a better sound to Linden's ears. But we'll feed them well, and send them off with good gifts, just as we ought."

"Will I get gifts as well?"

"Aye, and others to pass on to your uncle, too."

"Will I get a sword?"

"No you will not! Wealthy though we are, we can't run to that sort of expense, my lad! Besides, I don't think we've anyone who could make you one, even if you did deserve it – and that won't be for a few years yet, anyway."

"What does that mean?"

Var looked down at her son. "Your fathir bought his sword from the proceeds of a lot of years' shipwork, and from what little his own fathir's shipmates brought back with them by way of compensation for the old man's death over sea. He's never had enough money to even think about having another one: it's more than even a blacksmith as skilled as Jon can manage, too. So we'll send you to your uncle with a spear or two, and the best knife we can manage to get. You won't go to him empty-handed, never fear."

"What about my dowry?" asked Elle suddenly, picking little Rowan out of the mud that began to ooze around their feet. "Don't forget that there's that to consider, and probably before he goes off to uncle Ragnar..."

"I haven't forgotten, don't you worry. And why do you ask?" Var smiled mischieviously. "Taking a shine to Onund, are you?"

Elle snorted haughtily. "I just want everything in place before anybody has to agree or make a contract about anything, that's all."

"But he's a fine enough looking man, for all that,"

prodded her mother. Elle had the grace to blush just a little.

CHAPTER FOURTEEN

"Your time seems to be very tied up with your people just now, lady." Onund sniffed appreciatively at the rich red wine in his horn as they sat around the hearth that evening. Around them, Linden had gathered a small crowd to hear her unexpectedly smooth voice sing of homes, lost loves and the ways of getting stuck in a midden. Hild and Ymma had retired back towards the looms and Kendrick had gone out for a bit of rough-and-tumble with some of the other lads from around the hall. Only Elle and Anlaf sat with their house-guest, whilst Yngvar stood by with their one and only small cask of that earthy, expensive wine.

"It's a busy time for them," shrugged Var. "It's not every day that a man gets the offer to go and be more than he can be at home. I've every confidence in Solmund and his bride: perhaps more than she has herself, but I'm sure that'll change as time goes by. We could never offer them anything like this; they'd be fools not to take the chance, and I've seen little if any of that in either of them."

Onund studied his carefully-trimmed nails, and then ran a hand through his neatly combed beard. "Do you not worry that you are leaving yourself short of good help, though, if only until your lord returns?"

Var smiled. "Not at all: Anlaf is here with his gang of lads, I still have Sigurd, my own equivalent of Anlaf, albeit not so well-connected in the wider world... and he bosses it over our own bondar, all of whom have never shown the slightest signs of any real dissent towards us. And then there's Asa, who shares Brynjolf's hall with him, and Thordis, whose estates border your own, I understand. So no, I don't think there's any likelihood of my being undermanned over the summer. Come to think of it, were I to need fighting men, I suppose I could always send a runner to Vigdis and her appalling sons – although the haggling and deal-making involved in that might also be enough to persuade me otherwise!"

"So we're never going to be short-handed," added Elle after a slight nudge from her mother. "Is that how it works between you and your neighbours, master Onund?"

"Well... some are more helpful than others, let us say: but my connections into Mercia also serve from time to time."

"And I'm confident you have ample men to honour any request in the other direction," smiled Var. Onund looked puzzled for a moment, and then answered, "there's never been any help asked for from them." And so it was that once more, Var went to her bed with more questions than answers.

CHAPTER FIFTEEN

After the customary three days, Onund and his companions said their goodbyes and made their way back towards Hrafnkelsby, their bellies filled with the food of their hosts and their bags just a little more full with the gifts Var had arranged to send them off with. The rain had gathered overhead as Var and her houseservants huddled by the porch of the hall, doing their best to keep under its protective eave of overhanging, shaggy turf whilst also appearing not to be. Onund and his men had no such choice, however, but they made light enough of it.

"I think your husband's sent some of his surplus water to help us homeward!" joked the master of Hrafnkelsby as rain ran in rivers down his cloak and collected in puddles around his ornately-stitched shoes. He looked across the yard to where Yngvar and Arnkel the woodsman held the reins of their horses. "How is it, lady, that your people don't seem to mind the wet?"

"Probably because they get no chance to escape it, sir!" Var smiled back. "I'm sure you'll have such types around your own hall."

"Around it is one thing, lady; I'm not so sure my mother would be as happy were they ever to come in!" Onund swung himself up into his high-fronted saddle with its ornate wooden bow, and kicked his feet into stirrups, so that his legs stretched out along either side of the animal's shoulders. He watched as his mates did likewise, arranging the folds of his cloak behind him and shifting his bright yellow and blue shield until it sat comfortably across his shoulder on its strap. The thralls and bondar stood back as he urged the pony forward, and with a cheery wave and that winning smile again, Onund departed from Lisceardr. Var and her own entourage stood and watched, although still trying to duck out of as much of the rain as possible. No sooner were the little troop beyond the infield, however, than most of the relevant folk began gathering in the hall, anxious to hear and talk over what had been said, seen and heard during Onund's stay.

"I'm not sure what to make of him," said Var as she dug the poker into the fire and stirred it up a bit.

"What I do know is that after three days in this dress, I've no idea how we're ever going to get the pleats back into it." She shot a meaningful look over the flames at Ymma, who sighed theatrically and made a face.

"We know he holds Hrafnkelsby," she went on, "and that's not a bad start to a marriage-contract. Or it shouldn't be: do we know anyone who's actually been that way and had a look at the place recently? How well does he keep it? And is it his, or does he hold it from Ingimund's sons?" She frowned to herself slightly. "I never worked out how to ask that one politely enough, and it wasn't for want of trying, either. Didn't he just say something about his mother running the hall? How is it that he's got his mother there with him? Is the actual estate hers, maybe? Which of them owns it, then? What if he's just her tenant, putting on airs for us?"

"Ah, but what if he's not?" countered Hild. "He did come with men who seemed loyal to him, and that's a hard thing to fake, after all. I didn't hear any of them saying anything suspicious or dubious about their lord; they even referred to him as either lord or master."

"Did anyone get much else out of them while they were here?"

"They behaved," replied Anlaf. "They were friendly, talkative up to a point; no more and no less than one might expect from bonded men guesting in a strange house and having been told to be polite." He shrugged. "If you were somehow expecting them to go deep in their cups and spill all of Onund's secrets, lady, I'm afraid you'll be disappointed. They looked around and joined in a bit, and commented that life here was not so different to home. We'd've had to work a lot harder at gaining their trust before getting anything more out of 'em – if there's more to be had, even."

Var looked around at the collected faces. "So is the general opinion that I'm worrying over nothing?"

Hild raised her eyebrows. "That's hardly for us to say, lady..."

"And yet I ask it. You've been with me enough years to know that I wouldn't raise the matter if I didn't want to hear what you thought about it."

"Well then, lady, I would say that Elle is still young, and that it is still early in the summer... and why rush her into marriage? It's also as you said yourself: there's nothing can be finalised without the agreement of our master your husband, and lord Oslac. These are early days, surely? Master Onund might have been the first to come and declare an interest, but that's not to say he'll be the last; and wealthy though he might be, he came with only his own supporters to back his words. Perhaps you would have felt happier hearing what sort of a man he was from his mother, or some other of his family: folk of equal rank..."

"And not beholden to him," Var finished the sentence. "I *knew* there was something that hadn't sat right! Thinking back, he was lavish in his praise of his own worth, but as you say, how can those words be trusted?"

"A word of caution, though, lady," warned Anlaf. "This circumstance doesn't necessarily mean he's lied to you about any of it. We do know that he holds Hrafnkelsby, and that has to count for something, surely?"

"He said his folk might have come out of Wessex

as if I were supposed to know that it meant something," Var said thoughtfully. "And another time, he mentioned another branch of his family who had lands within Mercia somewhere – but he'd not been there, not since his fathir's death. Thinking back, I wonder if he deems it unimportant simply because it's not his? And if – if, mind you – that's his way of thinking, I wonder which he values more highly: that which he has, or that which he is chasing?"

"Plenty of relevance to a potential bride in those few words," murmured Hild, with a sideways glance to Ymma.

"The more we speak, the happier I am that I'm beholden to wait on my husband's return," reflected Var. "he and Oslac can sort it out between them, and then Hrolf can settle down to bargain with Onund properly, if he feels so inclined. Mind you," she went on, "some might see it as a good reason to go visiting this summer. Onund has come to look us over and done it uninvited, too: he could hardly complain if we were to go and do the same at Hrafnkelsby, now could he?"

"His place lies just a short way from my own lord's holdings," ventured Anlaf, "as I'm sure you recall, lady. Your own people seem very capable here: there's not a lot for my lads and I to be helpful at, if I'm being honest. Were you to pay Onund a visit, might I offer our spears as your escort? And then you might consider returning home by way of Eyvindstoft, and we could go home too."

CHAPTER SIXTEEN

It must have been a se'en-night or so since Var's world had quietened again after the flurry of activity and disruption at summer's start; the days had begun to merge together once more, routines and patterns had reasserted themselves, and life had begun to feel normal again. There had even been some activity at the loom: the new warp threads were strung and the linen loops hung around those of them that were to be tied to one of the two heddles. Red wool was balled and ready to be wound onto shuttles; more of the same colour – well, more-or-less the same in that it was a reddish-brown in hue – hung dripping gently from pegs set at the top of the back wall for that purpose. More often than not, dust danced in shafts of sunlight as they lanced in from the passageway, beyond which the main door stood propped open to let some spring air into the place, and lamps glowed in the darker corners of the hall. Even the strawstuffed mattresses from the benches and the shut-bed had been taken out, shaken through and re-packed with fresh material and Lady's Bedstraw, which, so Hild claimed, helped keep the bugs away. So it was with surprise and a degree of annoyance that Var twitched on hearing a distant horn one evening, just as the tables were being set out for the night-meal. She glanced over to where Yngvar and Ymma were hauling the main pot into the hearth from its more usual place in the cooking-house: their faces no doubt mirrored her own.

"That sounds like trouble," she sighed, placing her cup carefully on the bench beside her. "Haven't we had enough visitors already this year? If this *is* more problems for us, I don't know how I'm going to break it to Anlaf. He's eager enough to be gone as it is."

"Some of his men might not be so keen to leave us," said Ymma quietly with a faint smile.

"And what, exactly, does that mean?" queried her

mistress. She peered through a sudden explosion of woodsmoke at the girl. "You haven't been getting up to things behind my back have you? Please don't tell me there's a bairn involved in any of this!"

"Not for me!" gasped Ymma, reddening. "But some of the other girls have been... well, getting used to having Anlaf's lads around the place, if you get my drift, lady. And some of them are rather fine to look at..."

"Oh Gods: *that* I do not need! Tell any of 'em who might have taken their... admiration... a little further to go and see Halldora before they do anything else! If anyone can put such matters right, she's the one, although I'd really rather she didn't have to. Those boys have been here nearly two moons, now... I suppose I ought to have seen it coming, but it would have been nice if someone had actually bothered to tell me about it getting more serious! This could cost lord Einar dearly in terms of gelds and payments to the families when he gets back... and he's new in the district and we're supposed to be his *friends!* Real friends don't let their serving-girls get over-intimate with other men's bondar..." she growled deep in her throat. "Anyone from this household who ends up holding a bairn through their own foolishness is likely to have it taken away and left out on the cliff for the Gods to have the last say," she said in a low, ominous tone. "I'll not feed them out of my purse: and you can spread that word around as wide as you like. Now get that pot on the flame, and see to the tables. Yngvar: once you've done that, I want you to go and ask some men to find out who's blowing a horn so close that I can hear it in here. Then come back and get on with your proper work." As so often, her gaze wandered back towards her loom, now hidden in the distance of the hall. "Ah well," she murmured, "at least this time we nearly got it started."

CHAPTER SEVENTEEN

"I know him," muttered Anlaf with urgency and worry in his voice. "I ought to: he and I have been companions almost as long as I've followed Einar. His name is Hallfred, and he ought to be with my lady. So why is he here?" His hand unconsciously pulled at his short, trimmed beard, and ran fingers through the bushier moustache that framed his upper lip. "I don't like this; I don't like it at all."

"I can understand that," agreed Var. "Unexpected messengers are rarely a good omen, after all! The thing is, perhaps, who is he here to see? You or I? Either will bring its own crop of trouble, I'm sure; it's more a matter of which is the worst, and for whom."

Anlaf turned to look at her. "Lady, if he is come from my own lady Thordis with a demand for my return, then I have no choice but to go. We've been eating from your stores for long enough, and you've had precious little to show for us being here; I can't think you'd be unhappy to see the back of us all."

"The word is that some of my women might be less than glad of your leaving – but I think I've nipped any trouble in the bud. Should any of the lads wish to stay on, they would have to show that they can actually be of some definite use around here; although now Solmund and Linden have gone, I can see a gap that a decent craftsman might fill." She filled their cups from the jug which sat on the table, and regarded its contents thoughtfully. "It's harder to imagine what your lady could want to consult me about."

"Maybe she's inviting you to visit," suggested Elle. "That would be nice."

"Yes it would," smiled her mother absently, "but there's been so much going on already since your fathir left that I'm not at all sure I'd be very good company! However, we ought to sit back and wait for this Hallfred to show himself and state his business, I

suppose. That would be the sensible thing to do."
Elle made a face to show her opinion of being sensible.

Halfred was tall and rangy; his beard, like his hair, was dull copper in colour and thinning rapidly, threatening baldness. He stood on the threshold of the hall, hesitating, until Arnkel and Skapti ushered him closer to the hearth. His clothes were caked in dust and dried mud; he went to try and brush some of the worst off, but thought better of it under Hild's disapproving stare.

With a look at Var for permission, Anlaf poured the man a cup – which he downed in one gulp. "My thanks, lady... sir," he croaked eventually.

Anlaf grinned lopsidedly. "Have another, if your throat's that clogged! But you don't get a third until you've said whatever it is that's brought you here in such a state."

That second cup lasted a little longer. "Our mistress Thordis sends you greeting, lady," Hallfred said to Var, "and to you also, old friend. She asks for your return to our household, and also, if the lady Var wishes, she is invited to Eyvindstoft – although the request has something of a sting in it."

"How so?" asked Var cautiously. "I've never known an invitation to guest anywhere to have conditions attached."

"It is not through rudeness, or any wish to give offence," Hallfred said hurriedly. "More, it is through my own lady's need. Sir, lady, we are attacked at Eyvindstoft. Cattle and sheep are being sent into our fields, and one or two of our own people have been driven out of those same fields by others – outcomers,

bearing weapons against them. My lady is new in this place: she's not so settled yet that she knows all of our neighbours, or even who to call on regarding matters like this. So she sent me to fetch you and our own men, sir, and to ask the lady Var if she would lend her own knowledge and expertise in dealing with this." He leaned closer and lowered his voice a little. "Between us, I think she is missing her own lord and husband enough as it is; these incidents have only made that feeling stronger. She could use a friend, lady, and yours was the only name she could recall, both from the help you gave when we buried the lord Eyvind and the knowledge of where her lord had set out for with his own followers."

"Then you can tell her I'm happy to come," replied Var. "Anlaf and his men can be my escort, and if we take just one or two of my own people along as well, they can come back with me – as well as lending a spear or two along the edges of your own lands." She steepled her fingers and rested her chin on them, thinking. "And while we're in the district, if I bring Elle along with me, we'll have a reason for going over to Hrafnkelsby as well."

"If there's vikings in the area, would that be so wise?" wondered Anlaf. "Although I do wonder how it would be that we managed to miss a ship heading into the river here."

"We wouldn't," snorted Var derisively. "That's why I'm sure it's safe enough to travel, especially for someone such as I, who's well-known enough in these parts to deter any attackers. These will be men from nearby... were you at the Thing? Oslac said something about one or two folk having been to visit him around the time Eyvind died. Elle dear, would you go and find Yngvar for me? Perhaps he can recall the names."

Anlaf watched as the girl untangled herself from her spinning and ran lightly out of the hall. "That to me sounded like a ruse to get her out of here," he prompted. Var smiled, but it was a tight, humourless stretch of the mouth. "One of the names *I* happened to overhear was Onund's," she said by way of answer.

"And if I'm right in what I'm thinking, then this is going to be an all-too-interesting trip to miss."

CHAPTER EIGHTEEN

There was activity all around Lisceardr, the Hall on the Rock. Men gathered belongings that, few though they might be, had somehow managed to scatter themselves all around the hall and into the houses beyond. Var took the big iron key that fitted the box padlock on one of those outbuildings, and sent one of her own in to retrieve spears and shields; some of her escort eventually showed up in the yard by the hall door sporting axes from their own woodpiles and a selection of knives as well. Whilst being the first to admit that they would do nothing to frighten a contingent of, say, Mercians out of Legacaester who might decide to come in an attempt to reclaim this little part of their kingdom, or even her own husband's crew of ship-men, she also had to allow that they all exuded a nasty air of mean determination, and that they held their weapons well. It was not so far to Eyvindstoft: even a force of men on foot ought to manage the trip within a day. But Var made no protest as concubines and wives followed them up to the yard and slung satchels of food and spare clothing over many a shoulder.

"How come you and Elle are the only ones on ponies?" asked Kendrick, from where Thurbrand was trying manfully to hold him back out of the way.

"Because we're the only ones with the wealth and importance to deserve them," answered his sister with a smug smile. Var raised an eyebrow and the smile vanished. "That is right, though, isn't it, mama?" the girl asked.

"Yes, I suppose it is, but it's not so polite to spell it out in that way."

"Is there a better way?"

"Probably not," sighed Var, conceding the point and suddenly not having the energy to argue. Across the way, Anlaf's own companions made a slightly better showing, but he politely waved Sigurd and the other local men to the front of the column. Var nodded her readiness, her bondsmen shambled out ahead of her, and the men from Eyvindstoft swung into place behind.

Kendrick had not been entirely right when he thought his mother and sister had the only horses. Other, swifter messengers had already left by the time he had wandered out of the hall, porridge still smeared around his mouth and traces of cream on his everyday shirt. Hallfred was on his way back to Thordis, bearing the news that her own folk were returning, and that Var was coming with them; Hrafn was on the other, more southerly road, heading for Thorstienn's *tun* and the hall of Oslac the Lawspeaker of Wirhalh. If anyone was causing trouble, Oslac would want to know, and Var felt it better that he heard the latest gossip from her than leaving him to find it out for himself. His first action would be to send out his own people anyway, with the mission of determining the truth of the rumours.

"Is there anyone else that could be called upon?" Anlaf had asked quietly, "anyone else who might be disposed to lend a hand to a new neighbour?"

"Gytha's too far away, and we've only just sent her some of *our* best help," mused Var in reply. "We'll be going into Brynjolf's lands anyway soon enough, and we can ask Asa when we see her. But she's in the same position as I am: her best men are away, including her own lord, so I've no idea what sort of strength – if any – she could lend." She rubbed her eyes tiredly. "I suppose it was only a matter of time before someone worked out that we were weaker over the summers, when the ship's away... but I'm not impressed all the same." She looked over towards Anlaf. "But neither will Oslac care for any of this, and we can be fairly sure of his weight being thrown behind your lady. That should be enough to bring others in his wake... many of the smaller landholders around here tend to cluster behind Oslac, mainly because it's one of the safest places to be. Whoever's behind this incursion evidently isn't aware of that."

"Or doesn't care..."

"Don't say such things. That's just a whole new nest of troubles."

For all that the morning was already well advanced, traces of mist still clung to the marshes below the ridge. Across its gentler north-easterly slope it was less, and Var could see their road stretching across the outfields and between the long, narrow strips of ploughed land her bondar worked, towards the river's mouth that almost cut off her lands from those of her neighbours. Her escort was ready; Anlaf and the others from Eyvindstoft were even more eager to set out, and put their feet on the road towards home again. Elle was perched on her own pony, sitting upright but looking a little uncomfortable, whilst her younger siblings watched from the comfort of Hild and Thurbrand's arms on their shoulders.

"Keep order while I'm gone," their mistress commanded. "Just keep everyone at their everyday work as much as you can, and move them around as little as need be, should you have to deal with anything untoward. Most importantly, if there are major problems – send a message. Although the Gods will hopefully be with us, and keep matters on an even keel." She frowned, and waved a hand impatiently. "I don't know... just keep 'em fed and keep 'em working! That usually works for me."

"Go safely, lady," smiled Hild in return. "We'll deal with things here."

"Good." Var flicked the reins of her own horse and slowly, a little raggedly, the procession started on its way to Eyvindstoft.

CHAPTER NINETEEN

The lady Asa stood by her carved and painted porch-boards as the travellers from Lisceardr wove a slow path through her homefield and up to the door of Brynjolf's hall. She was around Var's height, and in all likelihood not very much older than her: but her years in this place had not perhaps dealt with her so kindly in some regards. Her face, although still striking, bore lines of worry and hardship, whilst the hair that hung from the knot behind her head had slowly turned iron grey. But she stood upright, and held a horn for her visitor, whose main preoccupation was not how her hostess looked, but how she was intending to get down from her horse.

"Bad times when ladies of halls have need to go guesting," Asa smiled as Var finally managed to find the ground. "You look as if you've not done that for a few years!"

Var grimaced. "Horses used to be softer, I swear... someone help Elle down if she needs it?"

"Mothir!" came the embarrased reply, and the girl slid effortlessly to the ground.

Asa's eyes grew round. "That's never your Elle..."

Var's smile was a wry one. "As you say, dear, neither of us have done this in far too long! Yes, this is Elle... didn't that man of yours tell you she was at the Thing, fishing for husbands?"

"You should be careful at that game," observed Asa. "All too often it's the wrong fish that bites."

"We might have already discovered that," Var replied. "There's a chance that such adventures have some bearing on why we're here."

"Come inside, then, and be welcome here. Your man gave the message that you might not stay, but if we send another onwards to... Thordis, is her name? I can't remember... well anyway, if we tell her you're here, and that we're conferring on how best to go about things, then you can go onwards in the morning with any plans we come up with – and safe in the knowledge that I already know them, and will be ready to render whatever needs to be done." She paused for breath and grinned at Var, who was still rubbing her nether regions. "From the look of you, I'd say the last thing you want to be doing is getting back up on that horse!"

CHAPTER TWENTY

"So then," said Asa once the ponies had been sent to the stables and drink had been brought out for the men accompanying Var, "what's to do? We've known each other long enough not to have to stand on ceremony now – and also to know that neither of us leaves our hearth-side for anything less than childbirths or burials. I've heard vague snatches of troubles brewing out towards Eyvind's old place: that what brought you out from home?"

"In part," acknowledged Var, "although I had been thinking about going visiting before any of this blew up. But then I was reminded that Hrolf had promised Gytha some help over the summer, so there was that to organise; and then, as you said outside, we'd been fishing for betrothal offers for Elle here, and we got a bite."

"And you alluded to that bite having something to do with this journey," Asa reminded her. The woman's grey-blue eyes fixed Var with a strong, unyielding stare, the sort that only friends of long standing could ever get away with. Var sighed and shrugged.

"Onund, from Hrafnkelsby. He came calling a short while ago, and put a proposal forward."

"Don't know him," sniffed Asa dismissively. "What's he like?"

Var looked across at her daughter in the firelight. "Shall I answer that, or do you want to have your say?"

"It's hard to explain," the girl began. "He's handsome enough, and very charming... but..."

Asa turned that same appraising stare on the youngster. "But not the right one?"

"Yes... well, sort of. But if I can't point at anything definite, it's not so easy to argue against Fathir striking a deal with master Onund when the ship gets back..."

"But important that you do it nonetheless. This is the rest of your life we're looking at! D'you really want to spend that many years bound to the wrong man? Oh, I know you could separate easily enough if it came to it: but untangling the legacies always gets complicated, and I've known men get killed over it." She sank back into her own memories for a moment; her voice softened slightly. "I turned away four men before settling on Brynjolf: did you know that, lass? Any one of them would've given me a good home and steady living... maybe even children. But they weren't right, and I was my own fathir's despair because of it. But d'you know what?" She leaned forward to emphasise her words. "I've never regretted the wait: not once. So if your fathir only sees such things as just one more business deal, you shout and scream and get as difficult over it as you can! Because it ought to be a whole lot more than just business; isn't that right, Var?"

"Indeed. I got lucky too, after all. I don't honestly think Hrolf would do anything against *both* our wishes, somehow. But Elle's right about Onund: he's not right for her. He's..." she stopped, groping for words.

"Clean," supplied Elle suddenly.

"Nowt wrong with bathing, girl..." commented Asa, but there was curiosity in her voice.

"Fathir has smuts on his shirt sometimes, or mud on his hose," Elle went on. "His hands go in the fire, they chop wood... he does his work every day when he's at home, and his best shirt only comes out at Thing-time and feastings. Master Onund was *always* clean: no marks on his clothes, no hard or dry bits on his hands; his hair was always combed just so and you could always see the silver rings he wore because they shone so brightly."

"He was on what he'd consider a very important

visit," Asa pointed out. "In his place, I'm sure any man would have turned out in his very best linens."

"He said he was master at Hrafnkelsby," Var put in, "but he never said anything about how he ran it. I suggested that, were he to marry Elle, he might want to take up a share in the ship – and he said he didn't sail." She turned incredulous eyes towards her hostess. "Do you know any other man of worth, of our husband's ages, who not only doesn't sail now, but has *never* sailed? Where's his wealth coming from? And what makes having ancestors in Wessex such a special thing?"

"Complex questions," said Asa, "but still not the whole of the reason for your coming here. Interesting though it is to discuss Elle's possible betrothal – and I still can't quite believe this is the same little girl I met the last time, when we came to Lisceardr – such matters wouldn't have been enough to haul you from your fireside, now would they?"

"No," admitted Var, sinking back into her cushions and staring through half-closed eyes at the patterns in the firelight. "Especially not when there's still weaving and making tapestries to be done. But it is surprisingly nice to sit at someone else's fire for a change..."

Asa playfully nudged her guest in the ribs. "Oh all right, then," laughed Var. "Thordis, Einar's wife at Eyvindstoft, sent a message to say she was having border troubles: armed men driving their animals onto her lands. She sent a man to me because mine was a name she remembered, but I'm surprised that one didn't come here, simply on account of your being so near." She leaned a little closer. "Then I recalled that Hrolf had mentioned something at the Thing: something Oslac had said about men getting cross when Eyvind disposed of his goods so neatly that there wasn't even the chance of grabbing a bit in the upheaval. One of the names mentioned in that regard..."

"Was Onund?" Asa interrupted with a shrewd nod. "Brynjolf told me the bones of it as well. So there's the makings of a pretty little stew, isn't there? What's your position if it does turn out to be Onund behind these disturbances?"

"You don't need to whisper, lady," said Elle from across the flames. "I'd worked a lot of this out for myself: I went to the Thing as well, you see."

"You'll do well then, whoever you end up marrying," smiled Asa with approval. "Perhaps I ought to be asking you rather than your mama, eh?"

Elle shrugged. "I'd already said that master Onund wouldn't be my ideal choice for a marriage: there's something that's somehow not very nice about him, for all his good manners and fine showing when he came to visit. And if he's moving against his new neighbours at the first chance, what does that say about his intentions towards the rest of us?" She shuddered. "I don't want to end up just as a stepping stone to some other ambition of any future husband's, and I begin to think that's what I might be at Hrafnkelsby. But how would I find out for sure?"

"Only by taking the final steps that committed you to the contract," replied Asa. "If I were you, I'd take my time and look around a bit more. Didn't anyone else at the Thing attract your eye?"

"Onund never even came to make his introductions whilst we were there," Var put in. "That gets stranger and stranger, the more I think of it, as well. How busy could he have been?"

"I don't think he even stopped to play the games," added Elle, "although it might be that I was looking elsewhere and just missed him."

"If he wore his finery to the Thing as he did to our house, I don't honestly believe anyone could have missed him! Although I don't think he'd want to get it grubby by running around after a ball, either."

Asa smiled faintly. "Bet you'd give rather more to miss him now, though, eh?"

"Pointless asking for what we can't have: that way lies bitterness and lost chances," answered Var. "For now, the plan is to go and meet Thordis – I've never set eyes on her so far, did you know that? - and do what I can to reassure her and organise matters if they need it. She's a ship-wife, after all: new to it or not, she's one of our fellowship and we band together against troubles. Once that's done, since Onund came to visit us uninvited, I thought Elle and I might return the honour. Fancy coming along?"

"I'm not sure that Thordis would be best served by the whole of the ship-crew's wives descending on her together. It might be better for me to wait here, until you send word of what needs doing – although if you want to add a few more men to your little *hird*, feel free to pick some out from my lads. We have spears to send with 'em... as for Onund... well, I don't know. We have to suppose that even if I've never heard of him, he might well have heard of me, if only by way of Brynjolf. You're capable enough of poking your nose into his business: you might want my company, and I thank you for the offer, but you don't *need* me there. So on balance, I'll sit by my fire here and relay messages back and forth. If there is any news that you need to hear, I'll send it on, you have my word; similarly, if you find you have need of something, send a message and I'll do my best to get it to you. Right now, something is telling me that it would be wise to hold something – or someone – back for a bit."

CHAPTER TWENTY-ONE

The estate formerly owned by Eyvind, son of
Asleif – nobody had ever known his father's name -
was considerably larger than that of Lisceard,
currently owned by Hrolf, the son of Dubhnjal. Or at
least, it looked bigger; Var did wonder as her growing
entourage tramped into it, whether this feeling might
be more due to its flatness than its actual size. This
part of Wirhalh overlooked the big, brown river that
ran along the northerly edge of the land; its fields and
forests ran gently down towards its muddy shores,
with only a small lift out of the water and none of her
own home's high, rocky hills and salt marsh to face
the open ocean.
"That was another bad messenger we've had all too
recently," she murmured to herself. Anlaf, who had
managed to borrow another horse from Asa, just
happened to overhear.
"The one who brought you news of the lord
Eyvind's death?" he guessed shrewdly.
"I hold nothing against your own lord and his
lady," Var reassured him. "But we had known Eyvind
a long time – since we first made our home together
in these lands. He was shipmaster before Hrolf took it
over, you know; he was that when my father-in-law
met his death whilst out on the ship, but you'd have to
ask Hrolf for the details of it. I don't think I've ever
heard them."
"He was in a bad way when we arrived, but he
struck me as a good and generous man..."
Var snorted a laugh. "He was a womanising aleswiller
who would go to almost any lengths to start a
fight if he wanted one! But he was also gentle, goodmannered,
and yes, free with his wealth... he never
married, but then you'd know that already, I suppose.
And he always had a tale to suit the occasion, and he
could pick good women, even if he never bothered

about making any sort of legal arrangement with them. One of the things I think I'm going to miss is his feastings: they were always a good place to be."

"It sounds, lady, as if you were rather fond of him, after a fashion."

"Hugely: he was very much like Hrolf, in some ways. Polite, thoughtful, dedicated... but don't ever try to push either of them where they didn't want to go. Then he'd get hard, mean, stubborn, and be reaching for a weapon rather than stand and talk any more."

"Is this the lord Hrolf or the lord Eyvind we're talking about here?"

"Take your pick! Although Hrolf's getting a little more flexible these days: which might or might not be a good thing."

"Presumably that would depend on who he's talking to? I found lord Eyvind to always be considerate and as helpful towards me as a man with no leg to stand on could be." Anlaf paused for a moment, his face in a thoughtful frown. "Even when the pain was unbearable – as I would guess it must have been for a lot of the time – I don't recall him being short-tempered or impatient with anyone."

"Ah, now there we must be talking about Eyvind. Hrolf's got no patience whatsoever with things – or people – that won't go his way!"

People were starting to gather around them as the sound of their travelling-horns rang out across the meadows leading up to the hall. Anlaf was soon conversing with familiar faces, gathering news and opinions before he needed to confer with his own mistress, the lady Thordis. Despite her own gathering worry, the one that always invaded her stomach as she approached a new place or a new face bearing a status equal to her own, Var managed to hold herself back from asking him what his lady was like. Following his return from his old comrade's burial, Hrolf had said little about his time at this house; as a result, Var knew practically nothing beyond her hostess's name. But the initial signs were good: a woman stood at the doorway with a large horn in her hand, eyes fixed on their approach. Polished bronze brooches hung at each shoulder, just below the line of a rich red shawl that contrasted with vibrant yellows and pinks within the rest of her attire. Her hair hung almost as long as Elle's, and was of a similar pale blonde colour; only the very tips of her fingers could be seen beneath the pleats and folds of her under-dress. Across her breast, strung between those brooches, beads and other jewels glittered in the cloudy sunlight. As Var brought her pony to a halt just a few steps from the porch, this waiting woman stepped forward.

"Lady Var of Liseardr, I assume?"

Var managed to turn her dismount into a graceful curtsey. "I am she, yes."

"Be welcome here, lady: and accept my thanks for coming so swiftly." She proffered the horn with a broad, open smile. "I am Thordis, and I am just so glad to meet a friend at last!"

"Your hand is shaking," Var whispered as she took the horn and drank. To her surprise, it contained not the more usual ale, or even mead: this was good, probably Frankish, wine. Thordis's smile faltered a little.

"That's probably because I'm at the end of my strength over this business. I wouldn't have disgraced myself with cries for help if I really hadn't thought I would need such aid... but..."

She caught herself on the edge, Var thought, of open tears. This was bad.

"Be welcome," Thordis repeated after taking a deep breath. "Enter and share our hearth. There is water waiting, and then I'll tell you everything that has happened here."

CHAPTER TWENTY-TWO

"We've not been in this place long, as you know," Thordis began once her guests had been seated around the High Seat. Eyvind's hall was larger than the one back at Lisceardr, and more vividly painted around its walls; the ale-vats were bigger too, and more numerous, but on her previous visits here Var had never felt entirely at home. The place had always been clearly that of an unmarried man, and there had been little if any investment in those aspects of a home that spoke more of comfort and ease than they did of wealth and ostentation. But that appeared to be slowly changing; whatever her own views of how things were progressing, Thordis had begun to put her own mark on the place.

"Not even a year, yet," Var agreed cautiously, "and yet the hall is looking all the better for it."

"I cleared out a lot of the unnecessary clutter – although there were some parts I couldn't really do much about until Eyvind was properly and decently in his mound." Thordis reached forward to lay her hand on Var's. "I really did appreciate your help during that time: it eased the burden on us all considerably, and most of the women here had not been brought in for their sewing or their cooking. Then it was the Thing-time, and then Einar was away for the summer with the ship... and then the troubles started."

"That's not really a long time, though: what, maybe a moon and a bit so far? We still have most of their sailing season to go; it's likely to turn into a long summer if we can't get this sorted quickly. So: what sort of trouble, exactly?"

"I know it's not been very long, but it's that constant, continual sort of pressure that just builds and builds. Little things at first, like Thorgils finding sheep in the outfields that weren't ours. So he drove them back beyond the border-mark, and made sure they were some way in – but he never saw anyone out with them. And it happened the next day, and the next... and then one day he and another of our men here, Eyjolf I think it was, were set on by men with spears when they sent the bloody sheep back to wherever they came from. After that, it became a case of going out in that direction and finding these men and their sheep waiting for them each time. In another place, the same thing was happening, only with cattle. They haven't tried breaking the soil and ploughing it yet, but I do wonder if it's only because we're at the wrong point in the year for it."

"How far from your own *bere* are they?"

"Oh, Eyvind always kept his crops in the infield, and we've done the same. Not from any need to safeguard them, I think, so much as just to make it easier come harvest-time. So there's no danger to the wheat or the barley – yet."

"What about the border-stones? Would you know if anyone's tried to move them? It's hard to see what other purpose all this could be serving beyond an attempt to move the bounds of your lands, and that can't happen without all sorts of legal involvement. I sent a messenger to Oslac the Lawpeaker, by the way, at the same time as I sent Hallfred back to you to say I was on my way. You need to get him involved on your side in whatever this dispute turns out to be about, and you need that to happen before the autumn Thing. Ordinarily, Oslac would deal with your husband over such matters, but since he's not here..."

Thordis raised an eyebrow. "I might have thought that the Lawspeaker would have been quite used to dealing with ship-men's wives after all the years the *felag* has been running."

Var shrugged. "Usually, things are pretty quiet: Eyvind's death and your arrival have been the biggest news we've had in years! But Oslac is a fair-minded man: if there's trouble brewing here, he'll want to get it dealt with as swiftly as he can." She smiled wryly. "I don't know how closely you've examined this place, but knowing Eyvind, and knowing what Hrolf's like, somewhere in these buildings there'll be one with a big padlock on the door. And beyond that door will be spears and shields and other such things: enough that, should they put their strength together, our husbands and their bench-mates could put a serious challenge up against anyone causing them – or their families – even a mild degree of trouble. If for no other reason, Oslac will be keen to sort this out and bring it to an end. Our ship-men don't make much of their weapon-strength when they're home, as a rule, but those who need to know about it have never forgotten that it's there. It's just that whoever is behind these incidents hasn't got around to realising that yet. Or maybe he needs it pointing out to him."

"There's not been any messages from Oslac so far..."

Var waved a hand dismissively. "He deliberates for a day or two, and like as not he's got his own men out and about, digging up whatever he can for himself. He's like that. Then he might make enquiries as to just where the borders of your land ought to be running, and then he might well take it on himself to go and visit your neighbours even before he comes to hear your complaint. Oslac is a man who likes to know where he and everyone else is standing before he does anything. It would be all too easy to upset the wrong person and make things far, far worse, by acting rashly or hurriedly. We've known him a long time: trust him. He stood firmly behind your husband throughout the Thing this spring – you should have gone. We'd've found you and made you welcome..."

Thordis smiled bleakly. "Too much to be doing here, I'm afraid. But it's getting less and less as time goes on: most of the folk here lived under Eyvind and they know what's needful to be done. It's only his women and a few hangers-on that have been a problem, and even they're getting used to the idea that the old ways are gone. *My* husband has no need of extra bed-warmers, that's for sure!"

Thordis had a delightful laugh. Var thought that, with a little more opportunity, it could fill the whole of Eyvindstoft – and beyond.

CHAPTER TWENTY-THREE

"Is it always as hard as it seems here, to run a big house?" Elle's voice floated through the gloom of the guest-house, with overtones of sleep and rather more ale than the girl was used to. Eyvind's brews always had been heady, Var recalled a little too late; she ought to have warned her daughter – but at least here, there were no men in the shadows watching for a chance at a tumble as she slid into her cups.

"Do you see me having this amount of trouble at home, then?" she replied. The question had made her curious: or her own drinking had brought out a faintly belligerent edge in her.

"No, but when something unexpected appears, even at home, it can make you bad-tempered sometimes. Lady Thordis seems to have a lot more to worry over, and so I wondered if I would find it as difficult, when the time comes. That's all."

"Ah." Var's rising anger deflated instantly. "I suppose it depends on the lady, to some extent, although the people she needs to manage can make it harder or easier, too. We're lucky at home: your fathir and I, and indeed his fathir and mothir before us, put a lot of effort into finding good folk and then keeping them. Many of our older ones, such as Grim and Thurbrand, came at your grandfathir's call, and then stayed on when he died; those more of my age, such as Jon and Arnkel and Hrafn, came to us as a result of meeting your fathir on his travels. Skapti and Thorhall have always lived at Lisceard: they just stayed on when their own fathirs died, and carried on doing their work, too. From what she said tonight, I gathered that Thordis and Einar had a smaller house than this, somewhere to the north of Snorri's lands,

which must have put them up among the Westmorlanders, I'd've said. They left that house to come here, and they brought a few of their best people with them, like Anlaf: but they had to leave a lot behind, too, just to keep it running. Bondar and thralls don't like upheaval and change, as a rule: take 'em away from where they're familiar and they can be troublesome. And they had to keep that other house working, or someone else would have moved in as soon as they'd gone, and taken it – and its income – from them. So they came into this big place, where all of Eyvind's folk already lived and worked, and had their own ways of doing things... so no, it can't be easy for her, especially with her husband off for the summer so soon after coming here. It might have been better had he waited a year before taking up his bench on the ship... but then, who was there to take his place, and put in his share of the crew? That shortfall would've been enough to keep your fathir at home for the summer, and as a result we'd not have had the wealth to buy in what we usually do to keep us going over the winter..."

"So it's all interlinked, then?"

"Sort of, I suppose... Thordis's troubles with this neighbour or whoever it is might be seen as the price we paid for getting the ship out this year, perhaps; but if that is so, then we did the right thing in coming to lend our help, didn't we?"

"And we can go to see master Onund at home, too..."

Var smiled in the darkness. "You don't sound too eager, little one."

"If I'm being honest, I'm not. I keep thinking back to the lad we met at the Thing. He was nicer, in some ways."

"More your sort of age, too... and closer to us in terms of distance. Well, let's see how it goes: we might not decide to go on to Hrafnkelsby after all."

"If lord Oslac is coming to make sure master Onund is keeping to the proper boundaries, and needs a show of strength behind lady Thordis to back him up, we might have to, surely?"

Sleep, so close and beckoning with open arms, vanished. Var sat upright in her bed along the wallbench and peered across the hearth at her daughter.

"You catch on fast," she said after a stunned few moments. "How long is it since you worked that one out?"

"I wasn't sure where Hrafnkelsby actually was until we got here: then I asked a few of the farmhands while I was out exploring before night-meal. Master Onund and lord Einar share a long border, and all the troubles have been happening in the meadows where the markers stand. It would be difficult for anyone else to drive their animals over that border without master Onund getting angry over it as well – and he was anything but angry while he stayed with us."

"That's right enough: I hadn't wanted to tell you before we were certain, in case you got upset over it, given that he's already asked to be considered for a betrothal to you. But at the moment, it is looking more and more as if Onund is the one behind it."

"So all our problems *are* linked," came Elle's voice, now with a slightly triumphant note in it. "But if he's making problems for our friends and *felag* members, I couldn't possibly marry him, could I?"

"Oh yes you could," replied her mother grimly. "If everyone decides that the best solution is a closer tie between Onund's party and ours, it's the obvious way to do it. I just wonder and worry if he's already worked that one out, too," she went on quietly. "I don't want to turn around and suddenly find out that all this fuss has been over a lot more than just the ownership of a bloody meadow. Oh, how I wish your fathir was here with us..."

"So you could put your heads together and work out what's really going on?"

"And for the reason that he never travels anywhere

without a good show of weapons!"

CHAPTER TWENTY-FOUR

Oslac, Lawpseaker of Wirhalh under the authority and support of the sons of Ingimund, was a solidlybuilt man with a dour, squared-off sort of face beneath his grey-brown hair and beard. It was a splendid disguise for a wickedly complex sense of humour and a brain generally acknowledged to be more agile than any other in the district. He could be a good friend or a formidable enemy; and in his patrons he had ready access to the highest quarters of Mercian society as well. Few cared to even risk the chance of crossing him, and those few that had, in times past, were not to be seen around any more. It was with some relief, then, that Var and Thordis sat demurely, trying hard to hide their elation when his messenger was ushered into the hall with news of his master's imminent arrival at Eyvindstoft.

"If this alone doesn't put a stop to your troubles, sister, I don't know what will," breathed Var once the message had been delivered. "I can't believe that anyone would ignore such a hint as having the Lawspeaker coming here to back you up."

"I'll be happy for that," replied Thordis shakily. "What's he like? This is another of those moments when I really, really wish I'd made the time to go to the Thing after all. Oh, I know I met him during the business of Eyvind's death, but I was hardly at my best then, either." She sighed heavily, a sad frown settling over her features. "There seems to be a lot of that: times when I'm not at my best. I'd rather have it otherwise, and I'm sure that at times, Einar would prefer it so, too."

"That's all very well as far as it goes," cautioned Var, "but you can't always afford to be what those around you might wish for. There's still the farm to run, and food to secure, and cloth to be woven, and more; and a lot of the time while you're doing all that, your husband and his mates are away on business of their own! Let me put it another way: where's the point in wearing the beads he got you on the days when he's not at home to see them? Finery and other folk's expectations are best kept for when they're appropriate – like when those folk are there to appreciate your effort. For the rest of the time, I say they can want what they like. I'm in charge, and things get done my way. It's the only way I can see anything actually getting done when it needs to be."

"Isn't a visit from the Lawspeaker – a business trip too, mind – one of those special times?" asked Thordis archly, with a smile. "So: what's he like?"

"Stone-faced; formal, but likely as not to throw in a funny line just to see if you catch it. He's come to Lisceardr once or twice for feastings, and he's always been good company. But he's moved in higher circles than ours, if the rumours and tales are anything to go by."

"Really?" Thordis's eyes widened. "What tales?"

"Sister, you're worse than Elle!" Var laughed. "Well, they say he attended one of the kings in what's now the North Way: you know, where Sogn and Rangerike and Vik used to have their own kings, and now there's only the one. He was in the retinue of one of those, I heard, although I couldn't tell you which one. Some folk have wondered if he was attached to one of the kings who went up against the winning one, and had to flee in consequence... he's always been close to the Ingimundissons, but their fathir came here from Ath Liath, although that might not make it impossible, since I for one don't know where Ingimund came to the Irish town from. He certainly knows the lawcodes that he says came from those places, for what it's worth. But he never says much about such things; I suspect he likes to preserve a little bit of mystery around him. It probably aids his reputation!"

Thordis grinned. "He can have all the mystery and admiration he desires, if he can bring an end to these troubles of mine."

"Aye to that," agreed Var. "But he won't be so far behind that lad, either. We'd – or you'd – better step outside and await him."

"Hrodni," called Thordis to a girl by the fire, "go find the large alehorn, would you? Put the wine in it and bring my cloak, too."

"Aye, mistress," came the reply.

"We must have a few moments yet," decided the mistress of the hall, "I've not heard a horn yet." As the requested items appeared by her side, she pulled the cloak over her head and took the horn from the bondswoman's hands. "Nevertheless, I'm waiting outside. I have no wish to appear even slightly unprepared."

"Very wise," Var said. "A little time out in the cold is a small price to pay."

CHAPTER TWENTY-FIVE

"Ah," said Oslac as he dismounted from his horse and bowed to the women standing before him, "I see that alliances and friendships have already been forged." There was a twitch of a smile as he accepted the welcome-horn, and then a raising of the eyebrows as the contents poured sweetly into his mouth. "Perhaps I ought not to be so surprised that the affairs of the ship are mirrored on the land whilst it is elewhere."

He turned to Var. "Madam, how is it that a messenger came from you regarding this matter, and not from the lady Thordis directly?"

"Because, dear sir, she couldn't recall your name, and her worry was great enough to cause her folk to be sent to whomever she *could* remember!" came the smiled reply. "As I understand it, the only time she's met you was when Eyvind died, and that's hardly the best of times for memorising names, now is it?"

"But I have your name now," Thordis put in, taking one of the Lawspeaker's arms as Var took the other. "Be welcome here, my lord Oslac: come and warm yourself, and I can tell you the facts of the case. Then, hopefully, you will be able to see a way to conclude this business once and for all."

The interior of the hall, despite the extra lamps and candles put out in anticipation, was dark and gloomy compared to the brightly-lit clouds outside. As the three of them stood blinking in the entrance-hall, Thordis skilfully guided her guest around the upright timbers that shielded the ale-vats, and through the narrow entrance to the *stofa*. Warmth wrapped around them; the sting of woodsmoke replaced the shining sky as the tormenter of eyes. Oslac halted for a moment, gently disengaging his arms from the two women to rub his face and draw his heavy travelling cloak over his head.

"It has only been a month or so since I was last here," he said with a chuckle, "and one day, it would be nice to come without finding problems already sitting in the High-Seat!"

To her credit, Thordis caught the joke. "You would be welcome any time, lord," she replied lightly. "But if you didn't tell us that you're coming, we wouldn't have time to make a puzzle to entertain you, would we?"

"And I know you of old," added Var. "You've never been one to sit at your ease for three days, not in all the time we've counted ourselves as friends. Admittedly, it would be nicer to come and just find enjoyable things to do, but our wyrds seem to think that that's a bad idea, too."

"Hmm, indeed..."

Thordis gently took his arm again and steered Oslac towards the High Seat. He accepted the invitation to sit between its painted pillars with a grave nod of acknowledgement; ale was brought, along with fresh bread, butter and a little cheese; the fire was built up and fine, meaty-smelling steam began to rise from the iron pot hanging over the flames. As the Lawspeaker sat and sipped his ale, Thordis outlined the situation. Oslac sat silently, listening intently; Var and the others in the hall held back, just out of sight in the shadows.

"What we first need to do," he said at length, "is establish beyond any doubt just where your boundaries lie, my lady. Until we have that knowledge, any talk of crossing them is just that – talk. It is perfectly possible for you to know that your boundary sits, shall we say, along the line of a stream that leads into the mere, whilst at the same time your troublesome neighbour can know with equal certainty that it runs some way to the west of that stream...."

"I know where the tally-stick is for this property – the one you and I marked, along with Anlaf and

Eyvind, and the lord Hrolf – if that would help," ventured Thordis. "My husband keeps it in his chest - to which I have the key, of course. Won't that say where the lands end that we own?"

"I can't remember, but it can do no harm to have another look. What worries me slightly is that it's not beyond the bounds of credibility to suggest that, whatever the token says, Eyvind might have, shall we say, *extended* his property over the years, without anyone having much in the way of defences to stop him. So it might be that, regardless of the description on the tally, its equivalents for the properties around you might still say that your boundaries lie elsewhere." He ran a hand through his hair and exhaled heavily. "I'm beginning to think that we might have to defer the final decision on all this to the Thing in the autumn; it's likely to take that long just to gather all the evidence and the witnesses you're all going to need."

"Witnesses?" queried Var. "What is there to be witnessed?"

Oslac managed to replace a sigh with a brief grin. "My lady, you know how this works! Anything going before the *herred* court requires the sworn oaths of any number of freemen simply to confirm that there's a case to deal with in the first place. Our lady Thordis here, for example, would do well to have her headman Anlaf swearing that she and her husband are indeed the legitimate owners of Eyvind's own property, and that he witnessed the old man finalising the deal. Then she ought to have some of Eyvind's old farmhands ready to swear that he never extended the boundaries by any means other than fairly bought or traded for, and that those borders haven't changed in as long as they can remember. Those are the two important points, I think: that Einar is actually the legal inheritor of Eyvindstoft, and that the farm has stayed the same in terms of size and composition

throughout any living memory. If you can muster all that, lady, then it rests with your neighbour, or whoever is behind these intrusions, to try and prove he has some right to the disputed fields. He would need to show proof of some sort that his lands have been altered in the recent past – and I say recent because there's not been any of this trouble until now, as far as I've been able to discover, and if it were a long-running problem I would have expected one side or the other to have brought it before me long before now! Assuming he can demonstrate such a thing, he would then have to produce witnesses who would say that he had approached either yourself or Eyvind about getting some sort of redress for his losses."
Thordis snorted. "Well *that* certainly hasn't happened! If it had, at least I'd have some idea of who was behind it!"
"All of which suggests to me that there isn't any legal basis for what's been going on," confirmed Oslac, nodding sagely. "This is a land-grab, a chance to try and take something while the men are safely away and the perpetrator thinks he only has the newly-installed lady of the house to deal with. Sadly for him," he smiled, "you had already made the acquaintance of the lady of Lisceardr!"
"So, given that you carry most people's boundary lines in your head," said Var, "who would you think is the most likely culprit?"
"Oh that's not so hard: it could be few men other than Onund, but then I suspect you'd worked that one out for yourselves," replied the Lawspeaker. "You'll recall that he was trying to stir something up about this just before our last Thing; your husband and the lord Brynjolf managed to separate some of his benchmates from him, which rather ruined his hopes, I think. I'd hoped that he would learn wisdom and leave it there, but it seems that I was mistaken."
"He came to Lisceardr to bargain for a betrothal to

Elle, too."

Oslac sat a little more upright and raised an eyebrow. "Did he, now? Well, that's interesting." But despite entreaties to say more on the matter, he fell silent for a short while.

"I think that while I am here, I might take the time to ride your boundaries with you tomorrow, my lady," he said eventually. "Then I can refresh my memory as to the precise details of your holding, and see what evidence there might be on the ground to back your position." He cocked a humourous eye towards Thordis. "Regardless of my lady Var here, I take it your previous lodgers have vacated the guest-house?"

"We had to put Eyvind in there for a night or two after he was dead," whispered Thordis ashamedly. "There wasn't anywhere else! And then Einar invited the Lawspeaker to stay..."

"I'm also going to assume that the old lord is satisfied in his mound? Not taking walks around his old house at all?"

"Not that I'm aware of, so I'm fairly sure he's happy enough in there."

"Hmm. I just thought that, if he wasn't, perhaps we might aim his steps in the direction of Hrafnkelsby!"

CHAPTER TWENTY-SIX

The wind was a little warmer on the following morning, although still strong enough to send cloaks billowing out behind their wearers and chill enough to make a return to the warmth of the *stofa* a cheery proposition. Despite the inconvenience and discomfort, however, three figures sat on their ponies at the edges of a meadow, with a cluster of discreetly-armed retainers huddled around them. To one side sat a thick, obviously ancient hedge of woven willow and hawthorn, settled snugly in the long grass around it and heavy with new leaves and the promise of berries come the autumn. At the point where the meadow turned a corner, a large upright slab of the local red stone, so easily carved but equally liable to be scoured by wind and rain, had clearly been in its place almost as long as the hedge. Oslac regarded the scene from under furrowed brows.

"Well my lady, clearly nothing here has been disturbed in either direction for quite some time," he said at length. "Are there carvings on the stone, would you know?"

"I can't honestly say that I've ever looked," Thordis replied. She glanced questioningly at the handful of men belonging to her own household, but there were no helpful answers forthcoming. Finally, Thordis slid elegantly from her saddle and picked her way through the long grass to look more closely.

"I can't see anything that resembles a carving," she announced shortly. "It's possible that some of the shepherds have put their names to it over the years, but there doesn't appear to be anything reliable, helpful or legal." She shaded her eyes with one hand and looked back at her companions. "So now what?"

"If this is where your folk say the trouble has been," said Oslac slowly, "then we can go along the hedge – which is as clear a boundary marker as I ever saw, by the way – and look for evidence of a forced way through it. It's not the sort of barrier men could just step over, after all, especially if they had animals with them. They'll have had to make a way through, and whilst it's possible, I suppose, to argue that men could go either way through it, nobody to my knowledge is accusing you of sending bondar where they ought not to be."

Thordis waited impatiently while her escorts sorted themselves out enough to help her remount her pony. From the way she had climbed off, Var was certain that she didn't actually need any assistance; but they were with the Lawspeaker as well as bondsmen, and matters such as custom and tradition counted as much in behaviour as in any other sphere. It was vital, after all, to maintain one's reputation and authority in front of either; and so Thordis waited until one of her men was ready to extend an arm to her and then lift her back into her saddle. That accomplished, the little group turned their horses and plodded slowly along the line of the hedge.

"There, lord..." one of Oslac's men pointed. Eyes followed the outstretched arm: the gap in the tangled stems was plain to see. In the slight dip at the base of the breach, hoofprints showed clearly in the mud, and they led from Hrafnkelsby into Eyvindstoft.

"How old are those marks?" the Lawspeaker demanded of his own followers. The men moved closer and bent to examine the track. "Days, lord, rather than any longer," one eventually replied. Oslac looked around the meadow.

"Well, there aren't any sheep wandering about in here today," he said laconically. "You men, get together and do your best to mend this gap. And if I make a token to remind me of when we did this, then I can count the days, and lady Thordis, if you send me word of when it is next broken through – on the very same day, preferably – then there is more evidence as to how often this is happening, and a clear sign of the offence being repeated *after* I became interested in it." He smiled faintly. "It's all good evidence for building a case on..."

"I am in your debt, my lord," smiled Thordis, more broadly. "Will you guest with us a while longer, and talk me through the whole procedure?"

"There are, sadly, other matters requiring my attention also," came the reply. "Much as I would enjoy a night or two here, I must head for home again. But you can send a runner if you have need, and if I find out anything more regarding this business, you have my word that I will send a message to you. By the time your lord gets home, we might, with luck, have this all done and finished with."

"That would be nice," agreed Thordis. "I'm not at all sure how happy Einar would be to come home and have this waiting for him."

Var shrugged. "He'd better get used to it," she said. "Homecoming hasn't been a quiet time for Hrolf in I don't know how many years."

"What of you, my lady?" asked the Lawspeaker, turning his attention to Var. "If you are returning to Lisceardr, coming by the southern road would allow me to provide some escort – and give us a chance to discuss a few unrelated matters."

"I mentioned that Onund had made a proposition regarding Elle," Var answered, "and I was going to use the opporunity of having come this far to go a little way further, and pay him a visit."

Oslac raised an eyebrow. "Beard the wolf in his lair, eh?"

"He came upon us unannounced, and uninvited, and I'd like to think we rose well enough to the occasion..."

Now there was a definite smile on the lawman's face. "And you're wanting to see if he can do the same? Little hope of that, I'd've thought, especially if he's in the market for a wife. That never augurs well, in my experience."

"He did let slip that he has his mother staying there with him, so there's still some chance. But we'll see; Elle's none too keen, and to be truthful neither am I. But this business has brought us this far, and it's the only chance I'm likely to get to see how he lives for real, rather than just havng his words to go on. Come the autumn he'll be back if he was serious about a betrothal, and then he'll be talking to Hrolf, not to me."

"Hmm. Do you not trust your husband to measure the worth of a man, then, lady?"

"I trust him completely in that regard; I *don't* trust him when it comes to judging what is acceptable in a house that my daughter might be taking charge of! It could be falling to pieces and Hrolf wouldn't notice; it need not have been swept out in years and he'd be fooled by the scents of strongly-laced stew and a decent vat of ale. Hrolf's a ship-man: providing the thing's not leaking directly onto him, he's not bothered. He can sleep anywhere, and at any time; cleanliness is a relative term, since he doesn't have a bath-house aboard the boat and can't be sure of finding one at whatever haven he fetches up in. No," she concluded, shaking her head for emphasis, "I can't – I won't – leave this matter to Hrolf alone. Elle and I will go and visit at Hrafnkelsby, and between us we can make a more-or-less accurate assessment of the place and its people."

"Well then, let me ask that you come by my steading on your way homeward, whenever that turns out to be," said Oslac. "My interest in this affair is growing, and by the time you have done your duty with Onund I may have more news for you."

This time, it was Var's eyebrows that lifted; but just as earlier, the lawman would say no more.

CHAPTER TWENTY-SEVEN

"There is some business you might be more able to conduct than I would," murmured Oslac that evening. The tables had already been cleared after the nightmeal, and Thordis had put out a fine set of horn cups for her guests to drink from. Around the hall, folk were pairing off, two to a horn, according to the strips of inscribed birchbark pulled from a bucket; *tafl* sets were produced from bags here and there, and the chinking sound of dice could be heard amid the low hubub of voices. Var was drowsy; they had all come from the chill of the day straight into the hall, where the hearth had been stoked high in order to stew the sheep in good time. She could still savour the pepper and the ginger on her tongue; the other herbs and vegetables had rather faded into the background of such a lavish – and delicious - display of wealth. Now she peered into the luminous depths of her cup, where sweet, smooth mead waited to run itself over her tastebuds. She liked mead; it tended to like her less, and frequently punished her the following morning. But she was a guest here: it wouldn't be polite to turn such a delicacy down, now would it?
"What sort of business might that be, my lord?" she enquired quietly.
"The information I am in the process of gathering regarding our friend at Hrafnkelsby will, by the nature of things, be incomplete," said Oslac tentatively. "it is coming from a number of places, but none of them are actually Hrafnkelsby, if you follow..."
"And you want me to come to you after I have visited there, and tell you what it's like and if there's any signs of Onund's being the instigator of our lady here's troubles."
"Precisely and accurately put, my lady. Providing you keep your men close about you and don't pry too obviously, I don't think there should be any danger in

it... he apparently has you lined up as future family, after all, and it would be odd indeed if he were to keep things from you – like, say, ambition, greed, dissatisfaction, envy..."

"I assure you, my lord, if it furthers Thordis' case in your eyes, and keeps him further out of my own household, I would be delighted to do all I can. And although she's asleep on her feet over there, I'm fairly sure I can speak for Elle as well. Should I call her over and put it to her?"

"I leave that entirely in your hands, lady," replied the Lawspeaker smoothly.

"Well, that's fine," agreed Var. "After all, it's nothing that we weren't intending to do at Hrafnkelsby anyway."

CHAPTER TWENTY-EIGHT

Whatever degree of nervousness and uncertainty Var had experienced on the approaches to Eyvindstoft were multiplied manyfold as she crossed into the lands attached to Hrafnkelsby. Now she and her companions were in completely unknown territory: the ship-men had never had much in the way of business in these parts, and the usual road into Mercian lands lay further to the north, on the line of both Brynjolf's Burgh and Einar's holdings. Hrafnkelsby lay slightly to the south, on the edges of a patchwork of common lands, smallholdings and tied farmsteads, all mixed in with forest and meres. There was little of the high ground that marched in two lines down the length of Wirhalh, and on one of which Var's own hall was sited; at this point, even the land itself changed its character and seemed to be trying to become more Mercian, stretching into a long, flat plain that only ended under the towering cliffs where Ingimund and his highest followers had made their own homes after the disastrous attack on Legacaester. Since the death of Ingimund, there had been a sort of peace between the two factions; nobody could deny that his sons had worked hard to regain the trust and support of the Mercian king, and then when he had died, they had accepted his widow in his place. But now the word was that she, too, was gone from this world, and nobody seemed at all sure about what was to happen next.

According to Holbodi, one of Eyvind's old retainers who offered to show Var's own people the way, Hrafnkelsby lay at the far end of a gentle road that ran broadly south-west from a crossroads somewhat beyond the track to his own dwellings. The little party picked their way along a pathway that showed little signs of use: grass grew across it, and puddles of muddy water splashed onto legs and feet at almost every step. Elle wrinkled her nose in distaste. "How can this be the main path into master Onund's holdings, mama? It's far too overgrown: even we're making hard going of it. How would Grim and his cart manage?" She looked around her at the birch trees that stood a short way back from the road, amid long grass and nettles. "This makes no sense to me."

"Perhaps he has another road to the south," suggested her mother, looking towards Holbodi for confirmation. But that worthy shook his greyed head. "To my knowledge, lady, this is the only road in and out. Certainly it's the only one I've ever used."

"So you come here often, then?"

"Once, lady, many years ago, before this Onund took the place on. I've not had need to go back since, but I can remember the way well enough."

"Oh, I don't doubt that," came the dubious reply. Var exchanged a look with her daughter, and they picked their way onwards.

Var's stomach churned at every step her pony took; it was all she could do to keep a civil tongue in her head as they moved slowly but remorselessly towards Hrafnkelsby. Ahead of her, Wulfstan's blowing of the travelling-horn did nothing to calm her nerves, and she began to recall why she didn't journey very much, as a rule. At least she had been to Eyvindstoft before, even if the owner had been different: but she had never been to this place, and she knew of nobody else who ever had, either. That in itself was strange: Onund might choose to keep to himself somewhat, but where did he get his workers from? He seemed never to have hired local lads at the Things, he didn't visit – or at least, not within Var's limited social circle. The closer to Hrafnkelsby they went, the stranger and more peculiar both the place and its master seemed to become. By the time an answering shout greeted the horn, her hands were clenched tight around the rein to stop them from shaking.

They rounded a bend placed in the path to avoid a heavy clump of hazel trees, and found the first signs of habitation beyond it. Wattle panels stood to either side of the track, and the woodland began to give way to outfields of long grass. From thinking back over the journey so far, Var reckoned to herself that at least some of these fields might well be the ones that led to Eyvindstoft. A small group of men leant on spears ahead of them; Wulfstan and a couple of her other escorts were already talking to them. Var swallowed her fright and apprehension: now she had to be the lady again. As she urged her horse onwards, the men knelt until a flick of her hand brought them back to their feet.

"Your pardon lady," began one, showing blackened stumps of teeth within a battered, somehow dirt-stained face that looked as if such were its natural hue. "We had no indication of your coming: I've sent a boy back to the house. Might we guide you onwards?"

Var nodded and inwardly smiled. They had managed to discomfit this place already, and they hadn't even arrived yet.

CHAPTER TWENTY-NINE

Hrafnkelsby smelled of dreams. Everywhere the visitors looked, there seemed to be signs that grand plans had been made, ideas discussed, and a start made on bringing them out of the realms of the mind and into hard, visible reality. But then, in every case, the work appeared to have stopped: there were outbuildings that were barely more than a course or two of stone, lengths of timber cut and squared ready for building with, and pathways cleared that led nowhere. Even those houses that were complete, and evidently lived in to judge from the curious faces peering out of low doorways fringed by dirty, frayed thatch, somehow looked squalid and uncared-for: as if their erection had been somehow more important than their maintenance thereafter. Much like many of the folk who were timidly clustering around her, Var thought to herself. She busied herself with not openly wrinkling her nose as these poorly-clad creatures came closer; her pony gamely struggled onwards through an increasing depth of mud on the road.

"How does he ever keep himself so clean if he lives amongst all this?" wondered Elle quietly, nudging her own mount closer to her mother. "This is not at all encouraging, mama; I'm not sure even you could do a great deal with this place, going on what we've seen so far."

"I'd say he avoids it completely," Var replied. "There's enough to suggest that he's got great and noble ideas, but nothing to say he can put them into practice... and that in turn says to me that he doesn't do much in the way of overseeing these folk." She looked around. "There doesn't seem to be much going on in any of these fields, either... so why would he be so keen to break into Thordis'? That makes no sense: they don't seem to be using their land here to any great extent. What good would having more do them?"

Elle frowned in thought. "Isn't it about sowing time?"

"It is at home, certainly, and it would be in more or less every other household I know; but here? Who knows?"

"Well I might not know for sure, but I don't see any signs of those fields having been ploughed, either."

Var followed her daughter's subtle nod of the head. Beyond yet another ramshackle length of wattle, all she could see was rough, uncut grass. In amongst it, she thought she could see saplings, young trees growing wherever their seeds had happened to drop. She felt her stomach lurch yet again, and there was suddenly a chill in her limbs.

"By all the Gods," she whispered, "there's *nothing* going on here!"

"And hasn't been for some time, I'd say," added Ketil at her side.

"Mothir, I don't want to go any further," said Elle suddenly. Her eyes were wide with fright and there was an unusual tremor in her voice. "I don't want to be promised to a man who can't even look after his fields and his folk... or even worse, *won't* look after them," she continued. "If this is how he treats his livelihood and his property, what does it promise for his wife?"

"If it were only that we had come for, dottir, I would turn us around and be gone from here," agreed Var. "But it isn't: I agreed to try and discover a few things for lord Oslac, things he wasn't well-placed to find out for himself. We've promised Onund nothing – and nor shall we, no matter what this business with Thordis might lead towards." She reached out a hand to her eldest child. "You'll not be bartered off into this, I promise you. I can't imagine your fathir would allow it, either, and we have to wait until he's home before we can do anything, after all. So let's go onwards, and be polite in our guesting – and keen-eyed in our watching and learning, eh?"

Elle exhaled heavily. "Alright then. Just keep reminding me that I haven't married him yet."

Skirting yet another unfinished outhouse, the little party had its first view of Hrafnkelsby's hall. Predictably, it was smaller than Lisceard; its roof was grey and shabby, which allowed it to blend into its surroundings in a way that Var's own house never did. What little paint remained on the baregeboards above the doorway was faded and dull; instead of Lisceard's bright and high gable ends, this house sported a hipped roofline, where the ends were folded over and met the roofbeam further in. Smoke seeped from all across the turf; Elle looked on incredulously and mouthed, "no smokehole?" in disbelief. The whole place was ancient, and tatty. Unloved was a word that sprang to mind: there was no pride here.

They pulled their ponies to a halt in the muddy space before the door, and waited. Sounds from within suggested that somebody was at home; the crowd of Hrafnkelsby's own bondsmen that had straggled along behind Var and her followers milled about, both embarrassed and curious as to what might happen next. After what seemed an eternity, the little door creaked open.

"Well," came a familiar voice, "here's a surprise!" Onund strode out into the yard, still spotless in his linens, his smile fixed on his face. "Forgive me, my lady: I had not had word of your coming. But welcome: welcome indeed to Hrafnkelsby!" He swept an arm round in a grand gesture of inclusion, and appeared genuinely pleased to see his guests. Var hesitated, confused; then, remembering her manners, she held out a hand and allowed him to help her down from her saddle.

CHAPTER THIRTY

The interior of the hall was something of a contrast to the rest of Onund's estate: the floor was newly swept and the wall-benches were clean and largely free of the unavoidable debris that tended to collect around everyday life. The extra stools were evidently kept scrubbed whilst the hangings, although old, showed signs of care and occasional mending; the hearth was piled high with wood and little lamps shone brightly throughout the room, illuminating clean timbers and bright paint around the High Seat.
"Oh," excliamed Elle involuntarily as they came into the hall, "this is unexpected..."
"But clearly where all the money and effort is spent," murmured Var in reply.
"I try to keep the place at its best," Onund was saying as they approached the hearth. "There's not many visitors as a rule, but I do think it important to keep a certain standard, as I'm sure you do, my lady. After all, you are the proof of my assertion, are you not?"
"It is certainly a noble place, worthy of royalty, even," replied Var. She found herself genuinely impressed: Ymma and Hild tended to only dust and wash in the most visible parts of her own hall, and saved the serious cleaning for maybe twice a year. This place looked as if it had been thoroughly scrubbed within the last se'en-night, and it had that air of this being its regular condition. Who did such things, she wondered to herself; the farm-hands outside didn't seem the types for it. So either Onund was a harder master than the road to his house suggested, or there was someone else involved...
"Do I remember you saying your mothir lived here with you, lord?"
"Hmm? Oh, yes... she's about somewhere. I'm surprised she's not here to greet you, actually..." the

shadow of a frown crossed his features for a moment. "She might have gone to rest," he decided after a moment. "She's not in the best of health these days, and she tires easily. Come, sit, and I'll have ale brought in."

"Where are the house-women?" whispered Var as their host went in search of a jug. "Listen how quiet it is in here..."

"Not like at home," agreed Elle. "This is creepy, mama; I don't like it at all. It's going to be hard not giving that away if we're planning on stopping for the usual three nights." She looked around her: at the tapestries running along the low walls, at the clean, rush-strewn floor under her shoes, at the strangely-swirling clouds of woodsmoke that obscured the rooftimbers above their heads. "There's no servants in the hall, and yet it's spotless... that doesn't make sense. What's going on? Is he a sorcerer, with an army of spirits to do his housework and keep him clean?"

Once, Var might have laughed at the idea, but sitting there in Onund's hall, the humour died in her throat. "Keep your wits about you then," she advised. "I don't think he's got the backbone or the strength for wizardry personally, but you never know. He did say his family were from Englisc stock, after all. I suppose that makes anything possible."

CHAPTER THIRTY-ONE

Onund's mother, it turned out, was named Alfwyn. She was a frail old woman, bent with age and a lifetime of hard working; her face was lined and grey, whilst her hair – what was left of it – spent its life under a heavy linen wimple. She wore no overdress, nor brooches or beads in the familiar style of Var's other friends and neighbours; her hands were blotched, gnarled and weak, the veins showing purple through thin, parchment-like skin. Where her son sported his finest shirt and breeks even within the hall, Alfwyn wore a faded, plain-hued woollen dress and worn, patched slippers. She also wielded a broom, and trailed a dusting-rag wherever she went.
"The closing of the day is not my best time," she explained as she served her visitors porridge the following morning. "My bones are getting old, and I need to rest even before the night-meal is done. This place takes a lot of looking after," she added, running a hand – complete with rag – along the edge of the nearest bench.
"I can appreciate the work involved," said Var diplomatically. Last night's food had been a stodgy, barley-based pottage, with herbs and onions. The bottom of the pot had charred slightly, and there had barely been enough to feed the three of them; no others had come in from the fields to eat, and Alfwyn had not appeared – and Onund had seemed indifferent to saving his own mother any of the stew. Var found herself repeatedly caught unawares by such behaviour, and as a result she was feeling the lack of sleep. There was no guest-house at Hrafnkelsby, it appeared, or at least no other accommodation had been offered beyond the benches in the hall. She was beginning to think that spending another two nights in such a place was likely to be the death of her, and the days in between were starting to fill her with dread.

"It must take a lot of folk to keep this hall so well," put in Elle. The old woman smiled.

"Oh, I manage, little one. It just takes me a little while, that's all."

"You... keep this place by *yourself?*" Var repeated slowly. She wasn't sure whether she was unable, or just unwilling, to take in the connotations of such a statement.

"I always have," replied Alfwyn. "It's my part of the arrangement that keeps us here. My son has his own duties, and between us we do well enough."

"I don't doubt that," Var hurriedly assured her. "It's just not what I thought to find, somehow, and I'm finding it hard to adjust to the new idea. Do tell me more: how, for example, would Elle fit in to such an arrangement? With a house kept this well, it's hard to see what she could bring into the place."

Alfwyn looked puzzled. "Is she coming here, then? My son hasn't said any such thing... or perhaps I simply didn't hear," she added quickly. "Well, another pair of hands is always welcome, of course... do you cook, dear? Onund is very particular about his food: he can get very ill indeed if he eats the wrong things. It's a constant worry, you know: he does so much for this household that the thought of him abed with sickness is quite frightening at my age. He drives himself so hard out in the fields and with his other responsibilities; he needs to keep his strength up."

"We must have fed him properly when he came to visit, then," replied Elle. "He didn't seem to be ill at all."

Alfwyn smiled, but the effect was more one of adding another crease to those already in her face. "I'm happy to hear it; he's far more particular about his meals when he's at home. But I raised him to be well-mannered and to behave in a way appropriate to nobility, so perhaps it's no surprise that he made such a good impression on you."

"Indeed," agreed Var smoothly. "His coming was quite an event, what with the ship having just gone out for the summer months. I do hope he was suitably entertained: we did our best, but it's hard sometimes to know what to do best for new friends when they visit."

"He told me that he was going visiting, but I don't remember him saying exactly where. But he came home safely, and we just got on with things much as before." As if reminded of something, she looked around the hall. "I'm not sure why he hasn't come in to breakfast yet; he usually has his porridge as soon as he rises. How odd... I'm sure it's nothing, though. Would you care for honey on yours?"

Onund eventually appeared around mid-morning, just as his mother was stirring the pot for the daymeal. By this time, his guests had inspected the tapestries which adorned the hall, and had been told at least three times that they were a lifetime's work, if not more so – some of the panels had been started by Alfwyn's own mother. They had looked at the weaving on the loom, and been assured of its quality, notwithstanding the fraying threads and the uneven tension across its width in places; apparently it sold very well in the markets of the Mercians, and was much in demand. They had helped wind balls of wool, and Elle had demonstrated her skill at spinning, much to the old woman's delight; she seemed to find it remarkable that a girl of twelve summers had even learned to master the spindle. Var decided that it would be impolite to point out that her youngest, Rowan, was just as good at it – and she was only six. And so they had processed around the hall, as if on some strangely miniature royal progress, and everywhere they went, Alfwyn's rag dusted and cleaned behind them.

"Mothir!" called Onund good-naturedly when he at last reached the hearth. Var couldn't help but notice that, despite having come in from outside only a short while ago, his shoes and hose were once again spotless. "Cease that: it's meal-time, surely!" He said it with a laugh, but Alfwyn looked as if humour was a stranger to her. She pottered over to the fire and gave the single pot another stir. "Have you bowls?" she asked her son innocently.

He scowled. "In their usual place, I assume."

Under the puzzled gaze of his guests, he turned to a basket pushed to the back of the bench beside the High Seat, and hauled it out. Alfwyn reached across and pulled out four wooden bowls, and spoons to match.

"We'll need the table out," she reminded him.

"Ah, yes: of course." He levered himself from his seat with what seemed like a prodigious effort. "Forgive me: habits are hard to break sometimes. Usually it's only the two of us, and we put the bowls on the bench between us."

"I suppose that with just the pair of you in here, your bondsmen make their own arrangements?" enquired Var.

Alfwyn nodded. "My son feels that their place is in their own houses outside, and it's true that they do mess the place up so, don't you find?"

Var raised an eyebrow. "I make 'em clean up after themselves... but lady, do you not have *any* helpers in the house? Not even a hearth-maid?"

"It's not our way," she replied mildly. "Onund prefers to be self-reliant in as much as he can. Many of the bonded folk around here are untrustworthy, he feels: dirty, unreliable types, with nothing in the way of the breeding or refinement that I tried to instill in him." She watched as her son struggled to lift the table-top from its habitual resting-place in the corner of the hall. "Sometimes," she murmured, "I wonder if he is really happy here – if perhaps he feels he has been denied greater opportunities, chances that might have come his way had we stayed within Mercian lands. Our family came out of Wessex: did you know? It makes us count among the nobility," she explained to Var's blank look. "Wessex blood has always been stronger than the Mercian: it's why that sickly king of theirs wed the blessed Alfred's daughter. To bolster the line, and strengthen them against the northerners."

"It's strange that you have been unable to attract suitable followers for the house," reflected Var. "I really can't understand why that would be... I'm not aware of any other halls experiencing that sort of problem. Oh, admittedly we have Thurbrand and Yngvar at each other's throats from time to time, and then there was that Welshman who came back with Hrolf last summer and has been an effort to control ever since; but the rest are happy and don't cause us any trouble at all, really. We've even had travellers come through and ask to stay: but that's more a case of taking a serious look at whether we really have any use for them. Might it be," she went on, as if struck by a sudden thought, "might it be that word of your being here has not spread far enough yet? Perhaps we had an advantage at Lisceardr in that my husband's parents had already established much of it by the time of their deaths: it might just be that word takes time to spread. I'm sure better men will come along."

"That would be a happy thought," gasped Onund as he set the board down and took a breath before going back for the trestle legs. "Don't you remember mother, what I said about the fine standards at Lisceardr, and the quality of the folk who had their living there?"

"I remember him saying how grand and wellordered it all was," Alfwyn said as her son stumped back down to the far end of the hall. "And I recall only too well how he grumbled about the contrast between your hall and his: how everything at your house seemed so easy and well-run, and how there was better food and good ale, and how the animals looked healthy and the fields were well tended..." Suddenly there was sadness in the old woman's face and bitterness in her voice. "I've tried my best to keep the house here, but it seems to get harder all the time: there's so much else needs to be done, and no hands with which to do it..."

"What about the men he came with when he visited?" asked Elle. "They seemed good, reliable types, well-paid and properly turned-out. Could not they take some of the burden from you, lady?"

"Oh, they're not ours," came the reply. Var raised her eyebrows in shock. "Oh no," Alfwyn went on, "my son arranged to have their company while he went on his travels. God forbid he should ever want to be seen in the company of our own rogues! What would *that* do for his repuatation?"

She laughed briefly, but the sound was brittle and could not hold against the return of Onund, struggling under the weight of six short lengths of wood and a handful of leather straps. In his presence, the talk perforce had to turn back into safer, more acceptable channels.

CHAPTER THIRTY-TWO

It was with barely concealed relief that Elle turned her pony out of the yard at Hrafnkelsby the next morning. Var had not yet got the full story of how she had managed it – if indeed the girl had had any part in the matter at all – but late the previous night, a man from their escort had been admitted to the hall to deliver a message purporting to be from the lady Thordis at Eyvindstoft, asking that her dear friend the lady Var of Lisceardr come to her as a matter of some urgency. Such a request could hardly be ignored, no matter what the conventions of polite visiting dictated; Alfwyn had been gracious about their leaving so soon after arriving, whilst Onund had hurried from the hall almost before the full message had been delivered. He had seen them off in a distracted and perfunctory manner too, with little in the way of gifts or words of friendship. In all, Var was happy enough to follow her daughter's apparent lead, and turn her steps away from Hrafnkelsby back towards friendlier shores.

"I don't know what you did," she said to Elle as soon as they were away from the edges of the infields and the trees began to crowd upon the track once more, "and I can't imagine how you did it, even if I can begin to understand why. But I suspect it's a trick to only be used in places like Hrafnkelsby; if you did it at, say, Brynjolfsburgh or any other of the halls we're friends with, it could place those friendships is considerable danger."

Elle frowned slightly. "I suppose then, mothir, that were I to say 'I don't know what you mean,' I wouldn't get away with it? I know that what we just did was the height of rudeness in some folk's eyes – but there was a reason given for it. It's not as if we just upped and left, is it? A friend sent word asking for our help, so we had to balance her need against our pleasure and the need won out. But did you notice that master Onund made no offer of help to lady Thordis? And he left the hall very swiftly once he heard who the message was from... I have to say, mama, that if what we did was rudeness, then so was his behaviour, surely?"

"Yes it was: and no, I hadn't noticed half as much as you seem to have – but then, perhaps you were expecting it and knew what to watch for, eh?"

Elle turned a slight shade of red. "I'm running out of ways to deny this, aren't I? But it got us out of that awful place," she added defiantly. "And I am truly sorry if I've put us at a disadvantage somehow, but I couldn't stay there any longer. I just couldn't!"

"I know," Var soothed, "and I'm as glad to be gone as you are. But I'm not so sure that we've learned anything useful to tell either Thordis or Oslac; it's possible that we might have left too soon, however hard the guesting was becoming."

"I'm not so sure we'd've learned anything more by staying," answered Elle defensively. "It didn't seem likely that we could ever get to speak with his bondar, he holds them so low in his esteem... and his mothir, too," she added with a shudder. "That poor woman... but if he thought to marry me just to take some of the burden from her, he'd have had a shock coming."

"I do wonder if a lot of her hardship's of her own making over the years," mused Var. "Your fathir and I made a choice when we discovered you were growing within me: we chose to rear you among lots of people, and not to do every last thing for you, even from a very early age, when you could barely crawl. It's taught you to do things for yourself, and having all the folk in the hall has taught you how to deal with people from all walks of life. I'm not so sure that Onund had any of that."

"It was all I could do not to laugh when I saw him having such trouble with the tables: when you think how easily any of our folk put them up and take them down..."

"He's one of those men who feel that the rest of the world is there to support them, and that they ought not to lift so much as a finger to get what they want."

"Is that a Mercian thing, d'you think?"

Var shrugged. "Perhaps: I really couldn't say, I haven't met enough of them to tell. Maybe you could ask your fathir when he comes home; it's certainly not very noticeable among any of our people in Wirhalh. I can't think of anyone who takes such a view of the world, can you?"

"Not straight away; they're all very practical and direct types."

"Well anyway, we're gone from there now, and I can't forsee any circumstance that would require us to ever go back. You've made it perfectly clear that you don't want his offer of marriage, and having seen how he lives, I can agree with you entirely! So we'll say that to your fathir and that ought to be the end of it."

"That would make me very happy indeed, mama. Could we perhaps arrange to go and visit beyond the Frankish place later in the summer?"

"The Frankish... ah, yes, the lad you almost snared at the Thing! Well, I can't promise: a lot rather depends on how this problem with Thordis runs. Our going to Hrafnkelsby hasn't really solved anything, or got us new information to pass on."

"Actually, mama, yes it has. Master Onund might not talk to his bondsmen, but I talk to ours. And they've got a lot more out of this visit than we ever would have."

CHAPTER THIRTY-THREE

"I can't believe you were already on your way back to me!" Exclaimed Thordis as she once more stood at her porch door, horn in hand. Var looked around her: this was more as it ought to be. Eager faces stood ready to take her horse; others waited to assist her in dismounting. Behind her, those who had formed her escort chatted happily with those who had stayed behind: all around, there was activity, talk, noise and the atmosphere of a busy, relaxed, confident farmstead.

"Trust me, sister, we couldn't wait to get away!" smiled Var as the two embraced. "You have Elle to thank for our swift return, although she declines to say exactly how she achieved it."

"Then I owe her thanks indeed," said their hostess, "but that's not what I meant." She leaned forward, her eyes wide and brows raised high. "There have been developments in the short time you were gone," she went on, "things said and shown that I can scarcely credit! You won't *believe* the half of what I've found out! So I was about to send a runner, and ask you to come back to me on your way over to the lord Oslac... and here you are, before I could even arrange it!"

Var took a step backwards. "That is... interesting, aye... and I reckon Elle has news for you, too, not withstanding her ideas about your neighbour which I'm sure will be highly entertaining! How do you feel about letting some of your bondar into the hall to tell their part of our little visit? I reckon everyone found out more than I did," she concluded ruefully.

Thordis laughed gaily. "Come inside," she said, "and bring as many in with you as you want! I never saw the point of trying to keep folk out, whatever their position; they all go to make the farm work, after all, and how else am I supposed to keep track of what they're up to?"

"That," said Var with a broad smile and linking her

arm into Thordis', "is exactly what I thought you'd say."

The *stofa* was as warm and inviting as ever: what it might have lacked in terms of cleanliness and illumination when compared to Hrafnkelsby it more than made up for in welcoming warmth and an all-embracing atmosphere of friendliness. This was a true living-space, the heart of the settlement – and it had been thus for many generations now. Var suddenly wondered whether Onund's family had been at his own hall for anything like that long.

"So then," grinned Thordis, looking more like a young girl discussing the eligible men of the district than the besieged, harrassed, insecure woman of just a day or so ago. "Who goes first? Well actually," she continued, "you ought to . Not only are you the guest in my hall, but some of my information isn't mine to speak, and the person providing it is in the guesthouse still. So then, how about we let Elle have her say? How did it feel to be dealt with on the same terms as all the other women in Onund's house? Think you could run the house with them under you?"

"There are no women," said Elle in a shocked whisper. "He sits in his hall with his mothir – and she does all the work! She cooks his food, she does all the weaving – and badly at that, for all that she seems to think it's a good cloth – and she cleans incessantly! I'm not sure that she ever goes out of the hall, to be truthful; she didn't seem at all aware of the state of the place outside. Master Onund tells her he has his business outside, and she accepts his word as it stands. And it's a mess, lady Thordis: there's fields left to wild grass and I couldn't see any signs of proper crops growing. None of the outbuildings seemed to have all their walls or roof on; I think all his bondsmen must have their own homes somewhere else, for he doesn't let them into the house at all. I had to take a real risk that the man I persuaded to bring 'your' message would even be let in..."

"Aha!" interrupted her mother. "I knew it!"

"I had to do *something*," Elle went on. "What little cash he appears to have spent on anything has all gone on the inside of his hall, and his bright, clean clothes. Nothing else appears to have had any money spent on it, and his bondar are left to their own devices – I wondered if that's why he can't seem to find as good a class of man as you and we do. And it's that part which I think has a bearing on your own problems, lady. It's my reckoning that his bondar have taken to bringing their own flocks – not his, for I'm not even sure he has any of his own – into your fields, simply because their usual grazing-places have been ruined by lack of care. He seems to have no interest in running the holding as a useful farm; he pays no attention to his bonded men, or to what they're doing. Were you to go over there and confront him with what's been happening, I'd put silver on his not having any knowledge of it."

"That's a lot to have learned in just a little time to wander around," said Thordis thoughtfully. "How certain of any of this can you be, my dear?"

Elle grimaced. "I spent almost all of my time with mama, as I ought to. But I managed to get out for a short while in the evening, and I took the chance to speak to our own men. *They* were pretty shocked at the lack of leadership in Hrafnkelsby as well, and so were happy enough to go around with master Onund's men to see what they did – all in a friendly and helpful fashion, of course. I doubt they've had time to tell me everything they found out: I would suggest, lady, that you call them in and hear it direct."

Thordis sat back in the High Seat and regarded the younger girl steadily. "I think your mothir ought to be so proud of your swift thinking and resourcefulness," she said eventually. "If you should decide that you'd rather be fostered than wed at this sort of age, there would be a place of honour for you at my hearth. I know that it's usually something that the boys do, but you are remarkable." She turned to Anlaf, who had been sitting nearby. "Was she this sharp in her own house?"

"Good at tafl," he replied with a grin, "and don't ever try to match her at riddles! And I'm sure I saw you at the fire as often as your mothir, yes?"

Elle blushed and looked down, which brought a good-natured ripple of laughter from those gathered around her.

"There was another thing," Var added as her cup was refilled. "When he came to us, Onund had good men with him – do you remember them, Anlaf?" Eyvindstoft's overseer nodded. "Well here's my tidbit," said Var, "his mothir says they're not his. He borrowed them for his visit: the only reason I can think of for doing that is that he had none of his own that he thought suitable."

"We didn't see any who looked especially impressive," Elle pointed out.

"So we are facing a man who puts all his efforts into making an impression that he can't maintain," said Anlaf slowly. "Furthermore, subject to what your travelling companions say, we have a lord who exercises no lordship over his followers, and takes no interest in running his lands. That's going to make it harder to bring any sort of prosecution against him, I'd've thought; but the lord Oslac is obviously the man who would know." He turned to Var. "Did I understand, lady, that you were intending to visit with him on your way back to Lisceardr?"

"That was the idea, aye. Now it looks as if it will have to happen, doesn't it? Sister, how well do you travel? I think you ought to accompany us on that journey, unless you'd rather try and persuade Oslac to return here... but I'm not so sure there will be much he can do now we've laid out everything we know, or think we know." She rested her chin in her hand, thinking. "What I want to know is where he got his travelling-mates from, because I recall them as being remarkably well-behaved and even deferent towards him. What does it take to have that happen when all I get even from Thurbrand is a grudgingly-given politeness as often as not?"

Thordis smiled her triumphant smile again. "There, I might be the one to hold the answer," she said smugly. "Anlaf, would you be so good as to send one of our lasses for our other guest? Inform her that we await her in the hall."

CHAPTER THIRTY-FOUR

The woman was around her own age, Var judged; she was reminded of Alfwyn in the Englisc style of dress, without the familiar brooches and beads, and with her hair neatly covered under her wimple. She looked tired, though, and the way her eyes darted around the hall gave an impression of insecurity and fear.

"Welcome again, lady Elfgyfu," said Thordis, rising from her place to welcome her guest. "Do come and sit with us: this is Var, the lady of Walea and its hall at Lisceardr, and her daughter, Elle. Sit, please, and be assured that nobody here means you any harm; we'll have ale brought, and the night-meal can't be far away."

This last statement was accompanied by a long, hard stare at the handful of bondswomen clustered around the other side of the hearth. Chains were duly rattled, kettles lowered, and lids lifted from bakestones to let the smell of fresh bread waft tantalisingly through the room. If Thordis referred to this visitor as Lady, Var reasoned, there had to be a reason for it. So who could she be? What relevance did she have to their current crop of problems?

"I'm happy to meet you," she said as Elfgyfu took a seat just a short distance along the bench from her. "Your name is not familiar to me, madam: have we met? Possibly we know you through my husband?"

"We have never met," came the reply: the voice was hollow and worn-out in its timbre, giving the sense of almost infinite sadness behind it. "There was no connection between us at all until earlier this summer, and had I had news of what was afoot earlier, I would have made the effort to come to your own hall in order to say what I have to say."

"I'm going to assume," said Var slowly, trying to feel her way into what was beginning to feel like a potentially lethal situation, "that you have already told some, if not all, of this, to the lady Thordis here; but I can't imagine what it is that you have to tell us. If there is no connection between us..." she threw up her hands with a laugh. "You have me, lady! I'm so busy trying to work out who you are and what your news is, and all I have to do is shut up and listen!" Elfgyfu smiled a tight little smile. "I can explain it all in one short statement, lady. I am wife to Onund of Hrafnkelsby."

Apart from a sharp gasp from Elle, the news was met with stunned silence. Even the sounds from the serving-girls had ceased – at least until Thordis, who had kept her smile firmly in place throughout, turned her head around and gave them another of her frowning stares. Satisfied that the usual routine had been resumed, she twisted back to face her guests. "Told you you'd be interested," she said with a grin.

"It was when I happened to hear that he'd been visiting at your hall that I felt urged to take action and bring my own tale to your attention," Elfgyfu continued. "I am wife to Onund, and I've been trying to catch you up for some days now. In the end I decided to simply come here and wait for you; lady Thordis was good enough to offer shelter until you returned."

"We've just been to Hrafnkelsby," said Elle. "Neither master Onund nor his mother made any mention of you, lady."

There was another dark laugh. "No, I can imagine that. But be assured, girl, it is so: I can produce witnesses to that effect, should it come to such. But I'm hoping it won't."

"So what exactly is your interest here, madam?" asked Var cautiously.

"That's simple: I'm aware that he's looking to take another wife, and in all likelihood place her above me in the household – although I doubt if anyone would ever be able to displace his bloody mother. Well, I won't have it: I came here to warn your girl away, and you too, were it necessary."

"Trust me," said Var coldly, "it isn't."

"No," came the bitter reply, "if you've just come from Hrafnkelsby I can imagine you've already seen enough; but if you have the interest, I can tell you a little more about my husband and his ways." She looked sharply over to Elle. "You've got a good mothir here, lass: and because of her, you've had a lucky escape. Had you wed Onund, you'd've ended up like his mother – and like me."

Var settled herself more comfortably on the bench. "We wondered how it was that the hall was so well-kept, when the rest of the place seemed so run-down."

"My husband is a man of grand ideas," Elfgyfu said sadly. "But he lacks any sort of energy or ability to bring them to fruition. The rest of the world can see it: more importantly, my entire family could see it when I couldn't, and they did their utmost to dissuade me from marrying. But he had such a smile, and such finery on him, and he spoke so well of all his accomplishments when he visited... and I never thought to question any of it. Tell me, lady, did he bring men with him when he arrived at your hall? Were they all brightly and impressively turned out?"

"Aye, that they were. We discovered from the lady Alfwyn that they aren't a part of his retinue."

"Retinue?" laughed Elfgyfu again. "He couldn't keep a retinue: he wouldn't know how! No sooner was I installed in the house than his mother appeared: it soon became obvious that he hadn't a clue about much of anything unless she spoke the idea to him, and explained how it worked. The place we had then was a well-enough estate: it was part of my family's holdings, and they put it up as my dowry. But he never came up with the bride-price in return; and then I found out that he'd never done a day's real work in his life. What was worse, he had no knack of handling the folk under us: those who dug the soil and minded the flocks and did all those other tasks that allow a house to run and prosper. I could do it: I'd been trained to it almost my whole life. All my brothers and sisters were: but he wouldn't hear of it. That was his work, or so he claimed; and I tried to be dutiful and respectful of my husband. So many drifted away... some of them had taken over from their own parents, they were almost a part of the family... and he let them go. He even evicted a few, I think just to try and frighten the rest into staying put. But it didn't work. We had to give it up; he was able to get us Hrafnkelsby somehow... I never asked for the details. I was just so relieved to have a roof over my head again, and I had hopes that this time would be better somehow. I think he held the failure of our old hall at Maserfieth against my family somehow: it was bad land, he said, and they had tricked him into taking it, and he didn't see how it could ever have given us a decent living. But others had held it before us: I can produce witnesses to that effect, too. And every time he found someone else to blame for these failings, there was his mother agreeing with him and telling him how awful it all was, and how he was always bred for better things... and how if they hadn't come into Mercia in the first place, they could have been the companions of kings and eorls by now. It was constant, never-ending; in the end I grew so sick of it that I had to return to my own people – or try to."

"They wouldn't have you back?" asked Thordis incredulously. "Even after all this?"

"They had tried to stop me marrying in the first place, remember," said Elfgyfu, "so I suppose they felt themselves justified in disowning me, somehow. Remember also that Onund and his mother had never paid over my bride-price either, and I think that counted against me as well, since if I hadn't been so set on him to begin with, they wouldn't have ended up out of pocket over it."

"I think I recall him mentioning another branch of his family with property deeper into Mercia," interrupted Var. "Somewhere near Wherington?"

"That's not his," snorted Elfgyfu derisively. "That's an estate belonging to my younger brother. But it's the one he fancied above the one at Maserfieth that we actually got. You see how lucky your own escape has been?" she asked suddenly. "Had he managed to pull the wool over your lass's eyes, you'd have been travelling my own road before much longer. He'd have come down to Walea and started eyeing up the parts he wanted... and as with my people, he'd've held out on his side of the deal until he got it, too."

"Or until my husband got tired of it and dealt with him properly," replied Var darkly. "What a tale... but what of you, madam? What are your plans? Do you intend divorce, since it appears to me that you've clearly already left his door? Is there anything we might be able to assist with, in payment for your information?"

"I won't divorce him," was the surprising answer. "I'm of Mercian stock, and a good follower of the church; one of my reasons for coming after you was to tell you that I wasn't about to allow a second wife in my household. I wonder if one of the reasons for Onund keeping the sort of company he sometimes does, and for coming into Wirhalh in the first place, was to see if he could indulge his greeds, for women as well as for other things. For all that he and his mother go on so about their bloodline coming from Wessex, there's a lot about your folk that he seems to find all too attractive. But the same principle that makes me forbid sharing my husband with another wife also makes me stay at his side, no matter how awful the treatment. We were married, and it was a Christian marriage, in the kirk, before God. I'll not be the one to call down His judgement by walking away from it, even if Onund thinks that living among..."

"Heathens?" supplied Var with an impish smile. "Damned? I've heard the words but I've no idea what they mean."

"You are kind," acknowledged Elfgyfu. "Yes, any of those would cover it, I suspect. Anyway, even if he thinks that living among those for whom such practices are acceptable will shield him from eventual Judgement, I don't. So I am happy to hear that you do not intend to let your daughter wed my husband: it means I do not have to be an enemy to you, and you've been kind enough to me even by just sitting and listening."

"My offer to help if I can also stands," Var reminded her gently. "Should your own position change at all, you can be assured of shelter and a welcome at Lisceardr. But if you do not intend separating from him, what do you intend to do? Go back? I can promise you only that nothing appears to have changed."

Elfgyfu ran a hand over her face. "I don't know: I've been moving so swiftly these last few days that I've not really had time to think at all. There's no welcome to be had from my own kin; I'm not so sure that there'll be much of one at Hrafnkelsby, either." She turned to Thordis. "Neighbour, I know you have troubles of your own with my husband, but you were good enough to give me shelter here. Might I beg it for a few nights longer? I'm sure you'll think it presumptious of me, but I really can't think what else to do right now. I need to sit and think, and at least while I'm here I might be able to repay your hospitality by lending some assistance in dealing with Onund and his bondsmen."

"From what you said earlier, it sounds as if he has never held on to good folk," observed Var. "The ones we saw around there looked to be the very dregs of the cask, and largely left to their own devices. We were even beginning to doubt if your husband knew what they did with their animals; has Thordis spoken to you about it?"

Elfgyfu shrugged. "I had an idea that it would be something along the lines of taking their sheep into other pastures: Onund never bothered planting anything, and he never thought to have the grass mown and put aside for feeding later in the year." She smiled sadly. "All he ever thinks about is his appearance and his mother's opinion of him. They're well suited in that regard: she has no time for anyone but him. That made my life no easier, either: she always took his side in any discussion, and he backed her decisions over mine. In the end I just gave up: I was treated like any other lowly bondswoman would be, and yet my background's a damned sight better than his."

"He and his mother claim descent out of Wessex..." Elfgyfu sniffed. "There's just as many poor thralls and cottar in Wessex as there are in any other kingdom,"

CHAPTER THIRTY-FIVE

The journey from Eyvindstoft to Thorsteinstun, on which estate Oslac maintained what most would consider a modest dwelling, was not so easy as that from Lisceardr had been. It involved either continuing eastwards until the traveller reached the crossroads that lay well within what was still Mercian territory and then striking back south until the old road to Legacaester met it. Then the journey turned westwards, through a number of farms and woods, until the more open expanses of the lands originally given to Thorstein – now long dead, of course – were reached. Alternatively, one could head back towards Lisceardr and Walea along the shores of the northern river, and then, rather than stopping to rest at the Hall on the Rock, carry on towards the south and finally turn eastwards, heading back along that older road from the other side. Both were long trips, and not designed for travellers in a hurry, for all that the old road still had most of its paving in place, and seemed to keep itself reasonably clear of debris. But there was also a third way.

The route Var found herself discussing with her escorting bondsmen even before the day-meal was served was not a good one. It involved narrow trackways, little more than muddy ruts in the landscape for the most part, that wound around fields and up over the rocky ridges that characterised the middle ground of Wirhalh. It involved skirting the very edges of Ingimund's original land-grant from Aethelraed the old king, and much of the land along that border was poor even by local standards: bog and mere and marsh, low-lying and often treacherous. Then the wary, and by now also weary, travellers would have to pick their way over rough ground where there was no road at all, and hope to drop back down the far side of the slopes, somewhere in the region of the Thing-place, from which it was a short and comparatively easy road to the house of the Lawspeaker. All her men spoke against it.

"It's bad ground, lady, with no clear road and very little in the way of help to be had, should we need it," growled Ketil unhappily. "Perhaps just as importantly, we would have no way to send a message ahead of us, and warn the lord Oslac of your coming."

"I can't see even that it would save us any time, either," added Hrafn. "The time it would take picking our way could be better used covering more distance on the established roads." He paused, eyeing his mistress carefully. "I'm even prepared to stick my neck out and suggest that our lord wouldn't even think of trying what you've suggested."

"The distance is shorter," persisted Var doggedly. "It's the shortest distance between this place and the place we want to go to. Yes it's hilly and sometimes hard going, but it's not like the mountains in the Welsh lands, now is it? There's not snow at this time of year, and it hasn't rained in a day or two... the ground should be fairly safe underfoot."

"Lady, that only makes it more likely that it will rain either today or tomorrow!"

Var eyed the little group of men coldly. "Are you saying – or as good as saying – that if I insist on this, you will not go with me?"

Heads turned to each other, exchanging looks and perhaps rather more. Finally, Hrafn spoke up. "Lady, though it grieves me to say it, if you insist on taking that route to the lord Oslac, then I would not go with you. But I can only speak for myself in this. I would do anything else you asked of me: were you to command that I go by this route on my own, I would do it. But you ask us to accompany you and the lady Elle, on horses where the ground is best suited to walking, and in a company where the way is often only passable by a lone traveller, and even then only with some hardship. These tracks are not kept open, lady: there's not enough use made of them for that. The nettles and brambles creep over them; the trees grow over and hang down, cutting out light and air. Foxes and weasels run everywhere; there might even be larger vermin about these days, for all I know. I really, really, don't think that we would all reach our destination unscathed if we went that way, lady, and that is my only concern in this." Around him, his fellows murmured their assent.

Var threw up her hands in defeat. "Very well then: I'm not so foolish as to try and argue against all of you. But the thought of going all the way into Mercia, almost to their city walls, just to turn back again, is enough to make me scream. That alone will take us half a day, if not more; Thordis and her lads here might not have that long before Onund starts making serious attacks against them. She's already sending them into the meadows with spears and knives; I reckon it's only days before this escalates into killings and compensations, maybe even outlawries. We – I – *have* to get word of what we've learned to Oslac, and then push him into taking some sort of action over it. I owe Thordis that much at the very least, not to mention Elfgyfu. Getting this dispute settled peaceably is the most important thing right now, and the road to that lies in getting what we know to Oslac as swiftly as can be."

"If you'll excuse my overhearing, lady," said one of the women tending the fire, "but there is a road that would save you most of that day you spoke of."

"Really?" Heads turned and looked over to the hearth: the speaker stood with a jug in her hands. "I don't know you, child," smiled Var gently. "Come over and tell us of this."

"I am Hrodni," the girl said. "I've lived here most of my life: my parents bonded themselves to the lord

Eyvind, and although fathir died some years back, mothir is here with me still. There is another road, lady, not used much these days but still passable, I believe. If you continue towards the Mercians from here, then just before you reach Ketil's pools there is a *rake* that runs to the south – and it's proper south, not westwards or eastwards of south, but south. That's the Welshman's road: it skirts around the city further along, and goes towards the hills of the Welsh lands. But before that, it meets the old road to the Thingsite, and so it takes you where you wish to go, lady. I hope it helps: I have no wish to see my hall-mates with wounds or punishments on them. None of this has been our doing, lady; we only want it ended."

"As do I," Var assured her, "as do I." She turned back to her bodyguards. "Well?" she asked with a raised brow.

Ketil grinned. "That sounds better, lady. That sounds like a road we can make better speed on than by going over the hills, and a road that we can do our duty to you on more readily. I'm in favour of taking that way."

"And are you all happy enough with that?" asked Var. "We haven't tested it yet: Hrodni dear, how recent is your knowledge of this road?"

"Folk from here use it regularly, lady: I can only imagine that the only reason nobody else has mentioned it is that we perhaps assumed that you would know of it already."

"Well I'm glad that at least one of you thought to pay attention and use your wits!" Var peered down at the strings of beads and trinkets spread across her breast. "Here," she said, twisting a half-coin from its wire loop, "this is for you, in thanks for your help today. Keep it safe, until you find out what it might buy you in the right places."

Hrodni's eyes widened; she reached out a trembling hand to take the precious silver. "You are very kind, lady," she whispered in awe.

Var smiled. "You were very kind too, dear. You had no obligation to share your knowledge with me, after all. Gifts should be matched, and I reckon half a day saved is easily the price of a half-coin in silver. Use that wisely, and it could be the start of great things."

"When were you wanting to leave, lady?" asked Hrafn. "It might take a short while to get our gear together."

"Been scattering it around the sleeping-houses, have we?" asked their mistress wickedly. "Just make sure you bring everything with you, then, and that you haven't left anything behind – like unexpected bairns. I can't imagine the lady Thordis would want to raise them any more than I would, and I would like to keep her friendship, thankyou. So if there's any of you been doing what your wives at home wouldn't like, now's the time to declare it."

"No, lady, nothing like that," she was assured by various voices. "Between going to Hrafnkelsby and heading back and forth as we have, it's not as if we've had a chance to get that friendly, either," Ketil added.

"Well I'm glad to hear it," retorted Var. "Go and make ready: I'll say my farewells to Thordis and then we can be gone. Oh, and find where Elle's got to, someone, and bring her back to me?"

CHAPTER THIRTY-SIX

Oslac sent men out on horses to meet his guests: this was not so much a show of strength or influence – although it naturally hinted at those and a good many other qualities – as a sign of his own eagerness to have them safely delivered to him in order to learn their news. Var had instructed Ketil quite carefully on the message he was to bear to the Lawspeaker ahead of her own arrival, and it had been with no small satisfaction that she had sat on her pony in the yard of Eyvindstoft and watched him gallop wildly off ahead of her. Now at last she too was on the final part of the road to Thorstein's *tun*, on a corner of which the lord Oslac, Lawspeaker to Wirhalh by authority of the sons of Ingimund, had his dwelling.

Oslac had no wife; he kept no sheep, and grew no crops of his own. His requirements for land were, therefore, quite minimal. But he kept a reputation, and that in some ways could prove to be a more expensive undertaking than farming, rent-holding or even ship-owning. He found it necessary to maintain a large and well-equipped following, and since he had to bring all his foodstuffs in from elsewhere, he needed barns and storehouses. So Oslac's steading was more crowded than many: buildings and sheds huddled together, making little alleys and snickleways between them. As their escorts guided them this way and that up the slope and then into this maze of structures, it became hard for Var to distinguish the workshops from the sleeping-houses. They were all of a similar size and type; most had walls of upright wooden boards, standing under roofs of turf, thatch or even wooden shingles. Var had never had an opportunity to visit the Mercian town of Legacaester, but she imagined from Hrolf's occasional descriptions of other places he had visited, that it must surely look something like this. Beside her, Elle stared at the

clustered houses in frank disbelief, and wondered quietly what anyone, even their Lawspeaker, could possibly need so many buildings for.
They eventually came to a halt before the porch of a house not so very much larger than most of the others around it. Var raised her eyebrows. "This is your lord's hall?" she asked the closest of Oslac's men. He nodded under his iron helmet.
"This was where we were instructed to bring you, lady," he confirmed. "It is where my lord always conducts his business, and receives the most important of guests."
"It would be nice to think we fell into both categories," she murmured. The man just smiled through his heavy russet beard, and beckoned to waiting lads for them to come forward and take the reins of the horses. Another of their company slid from his saddle and swiftly went inside.
His bench-mate watched. "Karl there has gone to tell him we've arrived," he explained. "It's not so often that our lord comes out to greet guests, so if you agree to it, lady, I'll walk you in."
"That will be fine," replied Var. "Oslac and I know each other well enough not to have to demand the niceites of visiting. Besides, on this trip it's business."
"Aye, he said as much." He reached up a hand to help her from the pony. "Will this lady be going in with you?"
"Yes, that's my daughter and she knows as much about our business as I do – if not a little more by now." Var reached ground and exhaled heavily. "It feels suddenly as if we've been riding forever."
"It can get that way after a while, I know. Well then, lady, if you are ready?" He put out an arm again; Var laid her hand over his and they walked to the door.
Lights were concentrated around a single table: there was, Var noticed with interest, no High Seat, or

at least not in any form she could recognise. There was none of the usual sights one found in other halls: no looms, no ever-encroaching mass of bedding and belongings, creeping forwards from the backs of the benches like some strange troll-creature looking for the light. There was a hearth, and the long walls had the familiar wide seats built along them; but there were no hangings to brighten the walls, no chains hanging from the roof-beams on which to put the cooking-kettles. This was definitely a place of work, and very particular work at that; but there were stools and benches drawn up around that solitary table, and there were large wooden chests, bound in iron, ranged around the room at the front of the benches. Oslac sat to one side of the table, cup in one hand and what looked like property tokens in the other. There were more tokens, and a few rolls of parchment, scattered around him. He looked up as they pushed the outer door shut behind them, and rose fluidly to his feet.
"My lady Var," he bowed. "Lady Elle too? Splendid; please, do come and be seated. Gisli: ale, if you would? And food: bring hot things. See if Lifolf has done cakes today." He glanced at Elle. "I'm thinking cakes might be better entertainment than proper food just now... or did you not eat before leaving Eyvindstoft? There ought to be porridge left if you'd rather..."
Elle smiled and bobbed a quick curtsey. "Cakes will be fine, sir, I'm sure."
"Your messenger hinted at much, but said little," frowned Oslac once the ale had been poured. "I gather from what you were saying to me at Eyvindstoft that you have since been to Onund's steading; from that, I infer that you have word of his involvement or otherwise in the problems of our lady Thordis. So: what did you find at Hrafnkelsby?"
"We found disarray and ruin," replied Var bluntly. "The fool is no leader of men, and seems incapable of

even the most basic of tasks. The bondsmen run their own lives; whatever he does when he puts a nose out of his hall does not appear to involve them at all. His fields are overgrown; Elle reckons that it's his tenants who are causing the trouble by driving their own sheep and cows into places where there is at least some decent grazing to be had. There's certainly none at Hrafnkelsby. But there's more: did you know he had a wife already?"

Oslac stroked his beard slowly. "No," he answered eventually, "that is certainly news to me."

"The lady Elfgyfu met us when we returned to Eyvindstoft," Var explained. "She... I'm not sure just what the position is between her and Onund right now, but she claims to be his wife, and wed in Mercia, under the eyes of the Mercian's laws, and in the eyes of their god. She was less than pleased when she realised Onund had come to Lisceardr in pursuit of a second wife: it's against their custom, or something..."

"And their laws," Oslac supplied. "The church forbids a man having more than one wife at a time. I can understand her upset if she's of Mercian descent."

"Ah, but so is he," Var went on. "His mothir, who is strange in her own ways, puts great store by their having come out of Wessex – although Elfgyfu sort-of suggested that there was less to that than Onund and his mothir are claiming. But the place is falling apart: all he seems to care about is the hall in which he lives – and only the inside of that, as well – and his own appearance. Having seen how he lives, and having listened to his wife's version of the tale, I'm not inclined to believe anything he told me while he was under my own roof."

"It makes everything just so much more difficult, doesn't it?" Oslac sympathised. Var stared at him for a moment.

"Actually, no, it makes my end of things a lot

easier," she answered. "Elle doesn't want the match anyway, and I've no faith that he'd ever put up the bride-price we'd be likely to set on her, either. He never paid it over for Elfgyfu, and he uses that as a way of blaming her family for all his troubles. They started off with property in Mercia, part of her family's holdings, but he let that go to ruin as well – and I've no intention of letting him come and pull my hall apart in such a way. The cheek of the man! I can't see what he hopes to have gained by any of this: we know what he is now, and if he was a stranger to most of our folk before, I can only see that getting more so as word spreads. But I suspect it will still need intervention from you, my lord, to bring Thordis' problems to an end."

"Well, as you know, I went in search of information as well," replied the lawman. "I discovered how it was that Onund came to Hrafnkelsby, and I found out who lent him the men that came with him to Lisceardr – did you know about that?"

"Oh yes," smiled Elle happily. "His mothir let it slip."

"But to be fair, she didn't know who they were *actually* attached to," amended her mother.

"That's where I come in," said Oslac, "but it's also at the root of much of what has happened this summer. I had better warn you now, lady, that there may not be very much that I can do to ease the burdens of lady Thordis."

"When we began to think that Onund himself might not be behind these intrusions into Eyvindstoft, we did wonder how much could be done," admitted Var. "But sir, we can't do nothing: even now, Thordis has instructed her shepherds to take spears and other weapons to defend themselves against further incidents. It's only a matter of time before we have woundings and deaths to deal with. Even if it's just a visit to Onund by you and your lads to make sure that he understands the consequences of what his own men are doing, it can't be just left to sort itself out!"

"And yet it might have to be," replied Oslac dourly. "As I was saying, I discovered where Onund borrowed his fine following from. You're not going to like what I found; I have to say that I wasn't especially pleased about it myself."

"Alright then," sighed Var. She was well aware that Oslac enjoyed his moments of surprise and high drama, and she was loath to deny him; but this was important. "Do you have a name? Could we perhaps send a few men his way, and try to... dissuade... any further support for this pretentious piece of shit?"

"It would take more than my few spears, lady, to accomplish that. His sponsor is Ingolf, younger son of Ingimund, in whose name I hold my position here. And so, at a stroke, my hands are pretty much tied."

CHAPTER THIRTY-SEVEN

Var stared at the Lawspeaker, aghast. "Ingolf?" she said incredulously. "Onund the do-nothing of Hrafnkelsby, is getting in with Ingolf? How in all the worlds has *that* happened? What could he possibly have that would cause someone of Ingolf's reputation to even notice his existence?" She looked around the room wildly, as if searching for answers, explanations, anything that might help her make sense of this latest turn in her wyrd.

"Well," she said eventually, "of all the things I might've expected to hear, that certainly wasn't one of them!" She returned her gaze to Oslac, who had sat silently as she absorbed his information. "So now where do we all stand? Regardless of your need to keep in with Ingolf as well, which I quite understand even if I might not agree with it in this instance, what's your view of this? Who's after what? It's hardly the sort of alliance I would've given any credit to."

"Oh, something's up and no mistake," agreed Oslac. "Whether these intrusions into Eyvindstoft are directly sanctioned by Onund or not, ultimately he *is* responsible for what his bondsmen are doing, and he's an even greater idiot if he thinks otherwise. But it might explain why it began in the first place: if he has found a way to worm into Ingolf's graces, he might consider himself protected against me – and thus against everyone else as well."

He sat back and closed his eyes in thought. "My belief is that some of this was started just a few months ago, when he came to me just before the Thing and grumbled about a lost opportunity to take a little more land into his own estate. I sent him away: I already knew that Einar was coming in, and that Eyvind had passed it all on to him correctly under the law. He never mentioned any friendship with either of the Ingimundissons, and so I have to assume that he's achieved that since our meeting. Ingolf can be easily swayed sometimes; he has an eye for the women, certainly, and from what you've said he shares that with Onund. And if you didn't know him, you might be forgiven for looking at Onund and assuming he had the wealth and depth to back up all that finery..."

"So he's been refused his wants by you and gone crying to the only people who could possibly have any power against you," Var summarised. "He's direct, you have to give him that, and it suggests a ruthless streak, too." She stared at Oslac for a moment. "What do I do if he gets that ruthless about Elle? If he has the ear of Ingolf and his crowd, why should he not come back to Lisceardr and just, well, abduct her? Where do I stand if that happens? Because I can't see Hrolf standing idle and letting it happen; I can't see Thordis letting Einar have an easy time regarding any lands taken by force from them over the summer, either. Gods, Oslac, he could be plunging half of Wirhalh into a war! Far be it for me to tell you your business, but you'll be forced into doing something sooner or later. Surely it's better to nip this early and avoid the ship-men rampaging through everyone's lands? If they get as far as the plains and the estates of the Ingimundissons, it'll be a bloodbath!"

"You think I don't know that, lady?" growled the Lawspeaker. "Onund has no recourse to the law – and he's found a way to thumb his nose at me over it. So I'm not happy at all about this either – any of it. He's a danger, and a danger of the worst kind: that sneaky, underhand, devious kind of danger that only has any right place aboard a ship!" He grinned to defuse the last few words. "My lady," he continued, "I am going to need a few days to consider this. I have to tread carefully, and choose my words well. I will send a messenger to the lady Thordis; in fact, I might send her a few useful spears, too. I think I can get away with doing that much and not be noticed... and I must send a rider to Ingolf as well, to find out just how much he has promised Onund in the way of support."

"You might want to ask what he's expecting in return while you're about it," added Var. Oslac nodded absently, already absorbed in his own thoughts. Var poured more ale for the three of them and motioned her daughter to wait quietly with her while the Lawspeaker groped for a solution.

CHAPTER THIRTY-EIGHT

There was little sign that her loom had grown any fatter in her absence. Var noted the fact absently as she finally settled herself back into her own High Seat and hoped her numbed, throbbing head might give her a little peace now that she and it were home again. Elle had wisely taken herself out to run around the yard for a while; there had been enough signs of her mother's growing bad temper all the way home from Thorsteinnstun. As housemaids, however, Hild and Ymma had no such chance to hide: their task was to report happenings and doings – or in the case of the loom, not-doings. Their place was to stand before their mistress and tell her all that had gone on in her absence.

Var closed her eyes and thought for a moment. Ingolf... she had been unable to get the name or its connotations out of her mind all the way home, and it was the primary cause of her current bad mood. What in all the worlds was Ingolf doing with a weasel such as Onund was turning out to be? It wasn't his sort of company, not to judge by previous rumours and stories at any rate. Ingolf and his brother moved in altogether higher circles; they mixed with nobility and even royalty when they could get a sniff at it. So what could Onund possibly give, when from his own wife's lips it would seem as if he were nobody important at all?

"Nothing about this makes sense," she murmured, more to herself than to anyone else. But Hild had sharp ears, and shot a questioning look at her mistress. Var sent a raised eyebrow straight back. "So tell me why there's been so little done to the weaving in my absence..."

"It wasn't for want of trying, lady," Hild began, "but you know yourself how awkward it's being this time around. Well, I can report that it has nothing to do with your own presence: it went just as badly for us as well!" She glowered down the length of the room towards the offending loom. "I'm almost at the stage of suggesting we get Halldora in to sing charms over the bloody thing; after two or three goes we decided not to waste any more time with it, and got on with other work."

"Your bairns are well and as full of energy as ever," chimed in Ymma. "Asbrand and his kin finally got on the road towards the lady Gytha, following Solmund and Linden, as you'd given them leave to do. There's been no fights, no emergencies... we must be getting into lambing-time, I'd've thought, although there's been no word yet from anyone." She spread her hands wide. "Quiet, for the most part, lady. How was your visiting?"

"Difficult," replied Var irritably. "There's no end of trouble brewing, and I can't be certain that we aren't involved in it just yet. So I need folk to be watchful for messengers, either from the lady Thordis at Eyvindstoft, or from lord Oslac the Lawspeaker. Or, come to that, from Onund, who visited us here not so long ago, although that's a message I might not especially wish to hear."

"Oh," said Ymma uncertainly. "Won't Elle be taking up his offer, then?"

"Ymma dear, I wouldn't send *you* to him even as a housemaid, let alone as a bride! He's danger and trouble beyond measure, and I'll be surprised if we've seen the last of him even yet. What's worse, we might not have much in the way of defences against him if he should come calling. But all that can wait: for now, we need food in the kettles and the fires making up again. I'm tired; if there's nothing that needs my attention straight away I'm going to ask for another cup and then I'm just going to sit here for a while, until my head stops pounding with the questions I can't answer."

CHAPTER THIRTY-NINE

"I've caught me a fine hare, lady..."said Thurbrand slyly the next day.

Var looked at him blankly. "Well I'm sure it'll stew up very nicely," she said nonplussed, "but unless you're wanting it to go in the hall's own kettle, I don't see why you're telling me about it." She frowned. "As it happens, I think Hild's cut up a sheep for the next few days. Your hare's likely to go off before we can eat it."

"Ah, but *this* hare's still jumping," grinned the cowherd annoyingly, seeming to join in with a joke that Var wasn't aware of making. "I'm betting he doesn't even realise he's been snared yet!"

A cold realisation began to dawn. "You said something a while back about setting traps for *people*..."

"Aye lady, that I did – but not just for sport, mind, and certainly not just to be cruel. No, lady, after my words with my lord your husband earlier in the year, I thought it best to gather a bit more evidence of my accusations before taking any further steps. But that gathering meant that I had to set a few snares, aye... and one of 'em's just been tripped."

Var sighed in the dark shadows of the lamps set around her loom; over to one side, Ymma and Hild were trying desperately not to laugh – too loud. Their mistress's eyes rested yet again on the cloth that seemed determined not to be woven this summer, and then closed as she silently sought for strength. "Come up to the High Seat," she said eventually, "and tell me plainly what you've done."

Thurbrand padded almost silently after her as she swept through the hall: but his shoes squeaked whenever he sprang forward on his toes, and his comb and knife banged on their tatty thongs against every table they passed. Eventually, Var slowly sat herself into the cushions of the High Seat. Thurbrand quite rightly remained standing until she waved him to a stool; from the corner of her eye she noticed Ymma standing with a jug at the ready. Var waved her forward all too eagerly.

"So then," she said after a long swallow of ale, "what have you done, and to whom?"

"It's that fat, lazy oaf who squats in your kitchen-house, lady, that's been the main target of my attentions," began the bondsman boldly. "As I told our lord, the fires in there have been stoked high on many a night – even after we've all done with eating and such, and even when it's not been a bath-night for anyone. Finding bits of wood that I'd put aside for something or other suddenly missing, well, that started me wondering. So I asked around a bit, and it seems that it's not only me who's noticed it happening. At that point, lady, I decided to get some hard evidence, something I could take as far as the Thing if need be. So I put some marks on some other wood, and I left it in places where it ought to have been safe: in stacks here and there, all tidy and obviously belonging to someone. Ever since then, I've been going around quietly and looking to see if they're still where I put 'em; most of them are, but just the other day I found one gone. So I went looking for it." Here he leaned forward with a triumphant look on his gnarled and weatherbeaten face. "And I found it."

Var sighed: she was tired. "It's been a long summer so far, Thurbrand," she said gently, "and I've had a lot to think about in all too little time. Right now, before more nonsense calls me away again without giving me time to rest properly, what I need from you is short verses, not whole bloody sagas! Get to the point man, and do it swiftly."

"I found my timbers in the kitchen-house woodpile," said Thurbrand shortly. "He was going to burn them in the fires, but I got witnesses there first, and they'll back up that my marks were on those pieces of wood!"

"By 'He', I'm assuming you mean Yngvar?"

Thurbrand nodded. "Yngvar the lazy, Yngvar the fat and idle... you know his own history as well as I do, lady. What sort of man is too idle to hold onto a wife and family, and would rather just let them drift away? What sort of man would sell himself into thralldom just to save the trouble of earning his own keep? That's what he did: all that and more besides. Would you necessarily call him trustworthy?"

Var considered for a moment. "I wouldn't put a great deal of trust in him, I suppose," she said reluctantly, eventually, "but then I wouldn't normally put anything especially important in his hands to begin with, either. This is different, though. He has his work in the kitchens because he's actually quite good at it: he can cook, and cook well, whatever the needs of the hall upon him. There are signs that he might be just as good at brewing our ale, and with Freydis not being so hale in her limbs these days, that's no bad thing – since you enjoy your beer as much as the rest of us," she added, nodding towards his almost-empty cup.

"There is a balance that ought to be kept up, though," retorted Thurbrand stubbornly. "We all have our work and our own skills, I know: but we're all here as a part of your hall, lady, and we all have to balance our wants against our needs, and those against the needs and wants of the hall, surely? I'd be so bold as to say that this applies even to yourself and the lord, lady: aren't there times when you or our lord have to put aside what you might want, in favour of doing what we all *need* you to do? My objection to Yngvar is that he doesn't seem to see it that way: with him, it's always his wants first. Freydis never burned the fires so brightly, or so late into the nights: what's he up to that she never was? Keeping himself toasted and warm, that's what! I'd go so far as to say that he's not even using the fires he makes for anything useful, and just keeping warm as an aside: I wouldn't object to that. But he's using up wood we can't replace, lady: we're not so well-off for trees or driftwood that we can afford this sort of wastage. And now I've proved my end of the accusation..."

"And so you want me to take it up from the other end," Var finished the sentence with distaste.

"With respect, lady, this would be one of those things I was speaking of – when your own wants must be put aside in favour of the hall's needs," said Thurbrand mildly.

Var scowled. "You set that one up very well, too," she remarked acidly. "If your other traps were as carefully made, I'm surprised that it's only Yngvar who's fallen into one." She sighed. "Very well, Thurbrand: I will look into it. But I can't promise when: I've been away from here more than I've been in. But you have my word: I'll take your words and actions, and I'll get to Yngvar about it. Because, I suppose, whether you're right or wrong in accusing him is beside the point: someone is using up the woodpile. And we do indeed have to find out who – and stop it from getting any worse."

CHAPTER FORTY

"Come to Eyvindstoft, lady!" The messenger lost no time in delivering his errand: he had barely crossed the threshold of Lisceardr before showing his token from Oslac and reciting his master's words. "My lord Oslac tells me that he will await you there, lady: he has further information to share, and the lady Thordis has need of any spare men you can bring with you."

"Do you have a name?" enquired Var wearily.

"My name is Ljot, lady. My father is Hallad, who farmed under Thorsteinn."

Var waved a hand towards another dusty figure seated at the table before her. "This is Erling, who has his living *at* Eyvindstoft, and who has just brought a very similar message! If people took the trouble to talk to each other before dispatching riders off at every wrong turn, I suspect a lot more might get done!" She smiled. "But that's not your business: come and join us, have a cup or two, and we can discuss what is happening in the east there a bit more closely. This hasn't taken me by surprise: I have my lads waiting only on my word, and after you've had a drink I'll let you both go so you can start heading homewards." She leaned forwards suddenly, catching the eyes of both men. "But I want one of you to go there indirectly. Now come, sit, and tell me what else you know."

"I know that my lord instructed me to come back to him at Eyvindstoft, but to go there by way of Brynjolfsburgh," said Ljot as he took a cup from Ymma. "Would I be right in assuming that's where you wanted one of us to go, lady?"

"Good to hear that Oslac is thinking a little more clearly than he seemed to be when I left him last," she replied. Ljot smiled.

"He was unhappy about many things for a day or so

after your leaving, lady: he hardly ate and we didn't see him at all. But then he roused himself and organised a campaign. I went with him to the lady Thordis; then he went onwards to Hrafnkelsby, whilst sending a couple of my bench-mates onwards to the lord Ingolf. Whatever business took him to Hrafnkelsby, when it was finished he went straight onwards; we only saw him again when he returned eventually to Eyvindstoft, and that was only yesterday. He set me my task at first light today... and here I am, lady. I was urged to make all speed, and to get back to him as soon as I might, carrying your answer and that of the lady Asa. My understanding is that others have been sent out to other households in the district with a similar message, but I have no idea what my master's plans might be."

"Bet you could take a guess though," grinned Erling.

Ljot shrugged. "If their message is anything like mine, then it's hard to escape the idea that lord Oslac is gathering the district's free landholders – and their spears – at Eyvindstoft in defence of the lady Thordis. My further guess would be that those spears are to be directed at master Onund in Hrafnkelsby, and that he seeks sanction for what he's doing from the Ingimundissons. But that's as far as I'm willing to go: my task is merely to carry the messages."

"And get back in time to carry a spear yourself," added Var. Ljot acknowledged that likelihood with a nod.

Var leaned back and sighed. "Well, you can inform your master that I will have around two dozen spears for him. I'll empty my husband's weapons-house, and

round up every spare man I can find, even down to the more reliable of our thralls – although I have doubts about the wisdom in taking such folk into a battleground, which is what Eyvindstoft is about to become." She smiled quietly. "I'm sure that while it's not what the previous owner would have wanted, he won't be too unhappy about it either."

CHAPTER FORTY-ONE

What Var had promised Ljot, who was now somewhere ahead of her on a faster horse, unencumbered by levied *hird-menn*, had been fulfilled. She had taken the big iron key, the one that was a little too bulky for even her to wear at her breast, and gone down to the little hut on the edge of the escarpment, a handful of trusted men in her company. Both Grim and Arnor, who were familiar with sharp implements, had come along, knowing full well that their age and the mysteries they wove around their pasts were likely to single them out for service in this adventure. Sigurd the overseer of Lisceardr was there, as the unspoken but acknowledged leader of the other bondsmen whose homes clung to the slope behind the hall, below their masters but above the fields they tended. Few of them sailed on the *felag's* vessel; Var wondered how many of them were suddenly wishing that they did. She also fleetingly missed Solmund, but there was nothing that could be done about that. Doubtless he had his own problems, and anyway, Gytha was too far away to be able to send any help in time.

They had found bundles of spears, their heads rusted and pitted but still able to take an edge. There were shields, for which Var was grateful: she had seen skirmishes in her youth, before she had come from Mann to this place, and she had seen the scarring and splintering of her father's and brother's war-boards. She had no wish to send her own people, no matter how lowly, into that sort of danger without even a shield to cover their torso. The memories were too strong, too vivid, and the wounds caused were often too severe to be capable of mending. Survival without a shield, she reckoned, was next to impossible. So the sight of a stacked row of them had caused a smile on most of the faces gathered there, staring into the dark dampness of the shed by feeble lamplight. Again, the conditions in the house had not been kind to them: many showed warping in their planks, and looseness in the rivets that held the iron straps to the back of the boards; there was more rust on the ironwork at back and edges, and over the bosses that stuck out from the centre. In places, the damp had got into the paint and glued them together; Grim and Sigurd had hauled the whole mass outside and set a couple of the thralls to separating them.

In one corner, under a handful of axeheads which Arnor had divided up with Grim in order to get them hafted swiftly, Var had discovered a tightly-wrapped object. It had been carried outside at her instruction, and careful hands had slowly unwound the linen and wool that bound it. Inside, they had found a sword – which was a mystery since, to her certain knowledge, Hrolf had only got the one, and that was quite properly on the ship with him. So whose was this? Its lobed pommel and narrow guard spoke of a degree of antiquity; the blade was stuck in the scabbard, which looked to be in danger of crumbling into dust. After pondering the matter for a few moments, Var had ordered it back into its wrappings, and then carried into the hall. Her husband could examine it, and shed any light he happened to possess, when he returned in the autumn. Right now, a single ancient sword was of no use to her.

"Not much in the way of bows," croaked Grim. Var shrugged.

"Hrolf's never been much of one for archery, but I'd've thought he'd have some in here, aye. Maybe he decided it was just too damp to keep them; or maybe he counted on everyone who had a bow bringing their own along. Sigurd, you might want to pass that word along; there's no arrows to be had out of here either, from the look of things."

"Aye, the air in here would play havoc with

bowstrings," agreed Sigurd. "I'll let the lads know, lady."

Var considered numbers in her head for a while. "We can call up a man for every spear in here," she decided in the end. "There won't be as many shields, but that can't be helped: much as I hate the idea, I'll not leave men at home for want of something to hide behind. So tell everyone that has a board of their own to bring it to the hall by night-meal, whether they get a call to service or not. Likewise with bows, arrows – I don't want to find even a single shaft left behind when we leave – and axes, and knives. Bring anything, everything... we can discard what we don't want, but only after we've seen it!" She turned to Arnor and Sigurd. "Think we can scrape up a score?"

"I would think so, lady," replied Arnor. "It's not really so great a number to find."

"I'm just hoping Onund gets left to stand on his own," came her muttered answer. "If he has to find his own troops, he's doomed, from what I saw. But if he gets Ingolf involved..."

"That would be a very different matter," finished Grim solemnly.

"And not a good one for us," agreed his mistress. "Not a good outlook at all."

CHAPTER FORTY-TWO

Yngvar the kitchen-thrall was, it had to be admitted, lazy: it often took the time and effort of another member of Lisceardr's extended household to extract a day's toil out of him. On the other hand, every time Var finally began to think that perhaps he wasn't worth the bargain they had struck a couple of years ago, he rose to whatever challenge faced them all, without prompting, without any sort of coercion. Like when the ship-men gathered every spring in readiness for leaving; at such times the hall was crammed to bursting-point with people, and yet Yngvar produced food enough for all, twice a day, with ale and milk to accompany it – and with only minimal assistance in the little house that held the main cooking-fires. If he then took a little extra wood to keep warm after the fires ought to have been banked over every night, Var would not really have minded so much; but he had got lazy and careless again, and now folk were beginning to notice. If Thurbrand had gone to the effort he claimed he had, then it must be getting *really* obvious.

The problem with Thurbrand, Var reflected, was that his own sense of pride and importance tended to get in the way of things. He was a freeman; no matter that he was a lowly one, with perhaps the most menial of jobs on the whole estate of Walea, it was the fact of his being free and carrying the knife that proclaimed him so that he centred on. Although Yngvar was probably far above his accuser in terms of status and the importance of his work to the homestead, he was still enslaved, and in Thurbrand's eyes, that made him automatically lower in the social scale. Var sighed to herself as she contemplated the short walk through summer drizzle to the kitchenhouse. To a great many folk, not just her awkward cowherd, that ladder-pole of relationships and relative worth brought all sorts of other assumptions and connotations with it. Thralls were at the bottom: therefore, they ought to be in amongst all the mud and the shit, literally as well as figuratively. Freemen rose above such things, in theory at least, simply by virtue of their not being someone else's property. The fact that most such men then needed to rely on someone still higher in the world to buy their skills and their time, and that some such dealings sailed perilously close to sending them into thralldom in all but name, never seemed to have bothered anybody. They were freemen: they had a voice all their own. Usually, that voice spent most of its time grumbling about the relative merits of those around them.

Var rather suspected that a lot of Thurbrand's anger at Yngvar stemmed from the thrall having found a warmer, cosier life than herding cows was ever liable to be. But saying so to either of them would solve nothing: that much was abundantly clear. She needed another approach.

She turned away from the rain hammering into the mud outside her porch, and meandered back towards the hearth of the *stofa*. Hild looked up from where she was packing wool away; today, the weft thread had broken repeatedly as they tried to pass it between the warps of the loom, and after a short run of such happenings, they had given it up for the day before anger took hold. Ymma was out somewhere, doing something or other: it might be a run to the well for water. Var hoped the lass had taken a cloak with her; in this rain, she'd need it.

She settled onto a bench just beside the High Seat and rested her head on the pillar. Closing her eyes, it felt for just a moment, did nothing to stop the racing of her mind, but at least it kept the smoke out of them for a short while. Gradually, she felt her body relax as she just sat quietly; the sounds of the hall faded away around her. What *was* she going to do about Yngvar?

"Lady?" came Ymma's quiet, hesitant voice. Var opened one eye: how long had she been resting thus, with so much still undone? Moreover, the girl was carrying another cup, and it did look tempting. But there was business to attend to first. "I need to go and speak with Yngvar," she said, waving the ale away and hauling herself upright once more. "I need to see how we are for stocks of things, and I need to have a look at the ash-heaps around his midden. And if you've just come in from the rain, then you need that cup more than I do."

Ymma looked puzzled for a moment; then understanding dawned. "This has to do with Thurbrand?"

"That it does – so not a word about any of this to anyone else, y'hear? The last thing I need is either for Yngvar to get tipped off and change his habits, or for Thurbrand to start hearing what I either have or haven't done as yet." She rubbed her face wearily. "I had less trouble raising the bairns, I swear I did. At least I could beat it into them that arguments and fights had better only happen for a reason!"

Ymma looked worried. "But if Yngvar's been running us low on wood..."

Var mustered a little patience. "Ymma dear, who else in this place cooks?"

"Me; Hild... ah."

"Now you see the problem! There's enough folk come to the hall for their eating that we *needed* to build that kitchen-house some years back: the hearth in here just couldn't cope, not with that many people crowded round it as well. Surely you remember: it was getting dangerous for everyone, and I at least refused to be knocked by accident into my own fire! So we built the kitchen-house, and took all the serious cooking away into its own little place. But the arseend of that arrangement is that, since we had a cookhouse, we had to put a cook into it: that was

Freydis, and she did very well. But as she got older and less able, we had to find someone else – and that someone turned out to be Yngvar. He started out in here, you know: but we moved him when he got in the way more than he helped." She frowned wryly. "Most of what you and I eat comes through his hands, now; oh, I know we put bread on the stones in here, and we have the porridge-pot in the embers most nights... but the day-meal proper and the night-meal come from the kitchen. I don't know how well he copes in there, but he's never asked for help, and in someone so lazy I'm pretty sure he would've asked by now, if he thought he could get away with it. But now folk are starting to notice the liberties he takes; and Thurbrand, for all his nasty edges, made some good and serious points. And so I have to go and find out just what he has or hasn't been doing; I have to hope he gives me straight and honest answers, and I have to try and find some way of keeping everyone happy." She looked at her housemaid. "I don't suppose you'd fancy trying your hand out there?"

To her credit, Ymma almost hid her true feelings. "If you send me, mistress, then I'll go," she said with only the faintest tremor in her voice. "But I've really no idea how well I'd manage."

"Hmm. All of a sudden I find myself missing Linden. Were she still with us, I'd seriously look at moving her into the cookhouse, with maybe you or Hild as company. But she's gone to Gytha," Var sighed, "and so that one's going nowhere. Oh, Gods guide me: I'm all out of ideas and I haven't even got to the bottom of the problem yet!"

CHAPTER FORTY-THREE

The kitchen-house was dug into the shallow soils of the ridge, as close to the end of the hall as could be managed. It still left a considerable distance for folk to traverse between the two structures, which with a full kettle or a hot bowl could be enough steps to court disaster. But since it was a later addition than most of the other huts and sheds clustered around the hall itself, its eventual siting had been a matter of taking what was available or facing massive – and expensive – rebuilds. Var waited until the rain eased before setting so much as a toe on the narrow, winding rut in the dirt that led the way to the cookhouse door. The building itself was more substantial than most of its neighbours: like the boatshed, its walls were of wooden staves, driven upright into the ground around the edges and secured to long sill-beams at top and base. The roof was steeply pitched, partly in an attempt to minimise the chances of it catching fire from stray sparks but mostly because it had just turned out that way; the rafters were covered in the usual turf. Within there was a large central fire, and a bench along one wall made by putting that wall out a little further from the edges of the pit that formed the floor. A couple of large vats sat in one corner, whilst bags and baskets piled up in every other nook and cranny, hung from pegs along every clear wall-space, and dangled from the crossbeams of the roof besides. The whole place reeked of bacon, onion, bread and woodsmoke, with a faint undercurrent of burning. It was also hot inside. Var could feel the temperature rising even as she approached the trio of stone-paved steps that led into the place, and she frowned. That didn't augur well for what she might find inside...

Yngvar was down to just a thin linen shirt, full of holes and covered in grease and soot; of woollen overshirt or breeks there was no trace. Yet even in this state of undress the sweat was running down him, and the fire was so bright it couldn't be looked at directly. Var stood by the doorway for a moment or two, trying to get her breath back; eventually, Yngvar turned and noticed her.

"Lady..."

Var pushed herself away from the wall – even the wood was warm, she realised – and forced herself to face her thrall in the middle of the room. "Yngvar," she began, "why is it so hot in here?"

The slave tried a nervous smile. "To keep the fires in, lady."

Much as she wasn't really in the mood for riddles, it seemed that she was about to get a contest. "Alright then: why is it needful to keep the fires in so high?"

"The kettles are big, lady, and made of iron, which takes a lot of heating. They get cold water put into them from the well, and that has to be heated to be useful, whether for ale-making or just cleaning the bowls from the hall."

Var growled in her throat, a sure sign of a shortening temper. "Other folk have iron kettles and they manage to heat their water and make their food without this sort of blaze sat beneath them! The lady Thordis at Eyvindstoft does all her cooking right in the hall, and she put food on the tables without putting so much fuel in her fires that there was a danger of setting the house ablaze!" She paused to wipe the beginnings of her own sweat-river from her brow. "Folk are beginning to notice what you're up to, Yngvar: already they are setting snares to catch you at thieving wood and peat from other places, and coming in here I can see no reason for it other than your wanting to stay warm the whole time! Now tell me this: what's in the pots here? It's nowhere near the night-meal yet, but the fires are stoked high enough to melt that iron you were on about... so what are you doing with all that heat, eh? Where's the profit or use in it for me, your mistress, eh?"

"I find it useful to be ready in good time, lady."

The tone was probably meant to be a reasonable one, but to Var's ears it sounded like a very unreasonable whine: the sort of tone men use to make excuses for their own failings. She set her face in the sternest of frowns.

"I won't have the whole farmstead in uproar over one thrall's behaviour," she said in a warning tone. "Either you get used to being cold again at nights and you take your need for firewood back to the level it always used to be at, or you come out of here and I'll find you other work. Your actions will determine what I do, Yngvar. Just remember that."

"Do I get a chance to defend myself, lady?" asked the slave carefully.

"What is there for you to say in defence of this?" replied Var in disbelief. "How are you planning to justify burning us out of a year's wood within a season?"

"I just get the idea that *some folk* have been making a bigger matter of this than it actually is," said Yngvar. "Aye, I put the fires high sometimes – but only when there's need or good cause, lady, I give my word on that. But I've been brewing the ale, and there's been a good few calls on the food-stocks since the end of winter, what with the ship-men being here for so long, and then that visitor from wherever he was from... in truth, madam, I've had to keep the fires in and keep them hot, or we'd all have been eating cold broth and bad bread by now."

Var considered for a moment. "When it was just... your accuser... grumbling at your master about things he couldn't get evidence for, I was content to let it go by. But now there is talk of traps having been laid – and of your getting caught with wood you weren't entitled to. And witnesses to the findings; so now I can't turn an eye away anymore. If there is much more of this, we're looking at either lawsuits at the Thing, over bits of wood of all things, or fights and assaults among my thralls and bondar – and if that happens then I have to side with the freemen, whether they're in the right or not. Because it's their voices that carry the weight in the Thing-court, Yngvar: you don't get a say. They have a value if they're wounded: you don't, or not as big a one at any rate. You sold all such rights when you took my silver and made your vows of thralldom to me; now you get to glimpse the price of the bargain, and I hope it holds your eyes well enough! So if there is any sense in that head of yours – take away their causes against you. Keep to your own woodpile; I don't mind if you go foraging on the shore or out in the fields to put more onto it, but don't you *dare* take any from the other stacks around here! And bank the fires over whenever they're not being used; I don't want to feel the heat as I walk past this place, and nor should I be able to. If you're really that cold in the night – which I doubt – go ask Hild or someone to make you another blanket. This has to end – now. You hear me?"

Yngvar bowed his head. "I hear you, lady," he murmured.

CHAPTER FORTY-FOUR

The road was a familiar one now: measuring its
length twice in a year made it almost commonplace,
reckoned Var as she trotted along at the head of
twenty-odd rather ramshackle spearmen. They were
not the best that Walea had ever fielded – but then,
the very best were out on a ship somewhere,
hopefully safe and well, and hopefully making more
of a profit than she seemed to be just now. All this
going here and there was exciting and interesting –
for her at least, since she wouldn't be expected to
stand in a line of weapons and shields and put her life
at risk for another's property rights – but it failed to
generate income. It brought in no extra food: in fact,
it had the chance of doing the very opposite, since the
men she plucked from the fields of Lisceardr could
not keep the weeds at bay whilst they had shields over
shoulders and sharp blades at their belts.
"I thought you'd not be far behind Oslac's man,"
announced Asa as the warband from Lisceardr
ambled – there was really no other word for it – into
her yard. "Come inside," she invited Var, "and tell
your men to make room among mine for tonight.
Then we can all go onwards together, and hopefully
make a decent show of it."
"Ljot said he would warn you of our coming,"
smiled Var as she slid from her pony. "I pulled twenty
men from the fields: how about you?"
Asa considerd for a moment. "About the same,"
she decided, "maybe a few more." She peered past
her guest at the knot of men resting feet, stretching
backs and flexing fingers after having them wrapped
around spearshafts for so long. "I take it you emptied
Hrolf's war-house, then? I've done the same here; not
for the first time, I'm grateful I married a man who
puts store by such things." She looked around again.
"How's your lass? What did she think of Onund?"

Var stared uncomprehending for a moment before realisation dawned. "Oh! You won't have heard, will you? We came home by way of Oslac's halls... well, step me inside, sister, and I'll tell you everything."

The next day dawned bright and dry underfoot, with a faint chilled breeze blowing in from the river. "Ideal for marching," commented Grim to Arnor. They were standing a short way apart from the rest of the men, leaning on their spears in the lee of the hall. Var raised an eyebrow. "You'd know about such things, then?"
"There's enough I've never told you of, lady," the older man smiled crookedly. "I can't really believe that this would come as such a great surprise to you."
"Oh, you're right enough about that," agreed the lady. "I'm more interested in whether you know enough to lead some of our lads, and whether you can run fast enough to keep up with 'em in a fight."
"Yes to the first, no to the second!" came the laughed reply. "I can walk unaided, lady, but I'm not sure that I could be fast enough in the thick of the spear-play these days."
"Then stay back," advised Sigurd. "Keep to the back of the gang and watch for weak spots: try and plug them if you can. I'll sort out two or three of the other lads who are getting on a bit as well, and you can stick together behind the rest of us."
"What, us younger and fitter types?" baited Arnor. Grim snorted. "Younger by a year or two, and as for fitter..."
Var joined the laughter. "Go get a horn or something before we set out," she advised. "The lady Asa says we can send ale down the line, and if she can arrange it, she'll bring a cask with us."
"I should've brought the wagon," reflected Grim. Var shook her head.
"You'd never have got to Eyvindstoft in time."

Whilst Asa and her handmaiden got themselves ready in the porch, cups were dipped into the ale-cask and sent around the assembling *hird*. The men of Brynjolfsburgh came equipped just as well – or just as badly, depending on one's viewpoint – as those from Walea: spear and shield were all that most carried. One or two, presumably surplus ship-men, sported leather hats, the hide sewn over a wickerwork frame to give resilience and strength; they all seeemd to have pulled on every surplus item of clothing they could find, on the basis that more layers might not actually stop a weapon from going into their flesh, but they ought to slow it down a bit, and make the wounds less deep.

"All the best men have gone to sea," commented Asa to Var quietly. "We've been left with the dregs, at least as far as wargear's concerned."

"It's never mattered before, though, has it?" came the reply. "And who could've forseen all this coming to pass, eh?"

"They're only bonded men and thralls," Asa went on. "They're the field-workers, the animal-tenders, the tree-smiths and shoemakers... those who had no wish for adventure and danger in their lives. They've got wives and children... and all we can give them is a spear and a shield." She turned suddenly to look at Var. "D'you know even how many of yours have *ever* had to fight before? Have they had any practice in how to do it? Do they even know which end of the spear is which?"

Var reached out a soothing hand. "Don't say such things in front of them, whatever you do... but I'm as frightened for them as you are. But we're their masters here: we have to lead them onwards, and we have to show just as much bravery and indifference as they do. It's going to be hard enough, I suspect, to keep Thordis showing her best front: but all three of us have to bond together here, and do our part. And that part is the one where we give the orders, and then sit on our horses and watch as our men get hurt and killed..."

"Don't say that!" hissed Asa. "This is getting hard enough already: I don't need you making it any worse!"

"Sorry: you're quite right. It doesn't help, does it?" Var looked across to see Nia's frightened face at the side of her mistress. "One of those special to you?" she asked in a gentler tone, jerking her head to indicate the swelling ranks.

Nia shook her head nervously. "Not to me, madam; but where I came from, this was an all-too-familiar sight. I lost all my brothers in similar matters... and then lord Brynjolf took me away from everything I knew. Seeing fighting-men on the doorstep is an uncomfortable memory, that's all."

"I thought you had kind words for one of the lord Hrolf's men when they came over last autumn," said Asa thoughtfully. "Sure there's nobody here who you'd rather not see heading into danger?"

"I beg you, lady, please don't taunt me so," replied the girl, with ghosts in her eyes. "Even if he were here, what could there possibly be that I might do about it? And what if he put himself forward for the duty?"

Var thought for a moment. "Ah: he was new to us then, if it's the one I'm thinking of. Erlend, we called him: we couldn't get a tongue around his proper name. He put himself into Hrolf's service when they clashed with that Welsh noble who has the lands beyond the Mercian bit over the river. I think he did it without bidding, too, which is odd... but he's not here, child. He's with his lord and yours, out on the ship. As a fighting-man, they decided he'd be useful; but it would've been handy if they'd left him behind all of a sudden, wouldn't it?"

"So you see?" chided Asa, "There's no need to fret

so. Now come along: get anything you need, and make sure I have my spare cloak and shoes. I find it harder and harder these days to be either cold or with wet feet, and I'm not going to arrive at our new neighbour's hall all shivering and damp! Oh," she called out to Nia as the thrall retreated into the house again, "and bring my strung beads – all of them! They're in a bag by the bed somewhere."

There was a muffled answer from beyond the door. "Bloody Irish," muttered Asa. "She's very good as a rule, and I'm glad I've got her; but I do wonder sometimes about how reliable she might be. If she's going to start casting eyes at every visitor we get come harvest-times, she might have to go. I can't – won't – have that sort of thing starting up; if she gets with child, how much use around the house will she be?"

"Hush," advised Var, "it hasn't happened yet." She saw no reason to expand on her own thrall's behaviour prior to his being taken aboard ship, or his obvious infatuation with the short, dark girl whose eyes seemed to see into other worlds at times. Let that be a problem for another day, she decided; they had enough here already. Nia returned to break her train of thought, almost buried under a large satchel, a voluminous cloak of grey Englisc wool and a very prettily-made pair of soft leather shoes. Asa peremptorily directed her towards the packhorses standing to one side; the two ladies beckoned to other nearby men to help them into their saddles. Once settled, Asa had a swift look around to ensure that all was ready, and kicked her pony to the head of the line. Another kick sent it trotting smartly out of Brynjolfsburgh, the bells on its harness tinkling as she rode, and heading eastwards to Eyvindstoft.

CHAPTER FORTY-FIVE

Relief flooded the face of Thordis as the sound of approaching horns was joined by the tramp of feet on dried dirt roads, the slap and bumping of wood on wood as shields and spears jostled with every step, and the sound of voices in both talk and snatches of song. As the men of Lisceardr and Brynjolfsburgh swung slowly into view, flanked by her own field-men as they ran alongside, it was all she could do to hold herself steady at the doorway. "Run inside," she instructed a passing thrall. "Bring me two horns of ale: we'll hold the wine back for later. I don't even know if the lady Asa drinks wine," she added as an aside to the Lawspeaker who stood just behind her. "Nor I," he replied, "although I would imagine that after a day on the road, they will all be happy to drink pretty much anything."
"I can put both on the table," Thordis decided. "It's hardly a problem to do it, and the least these folk deserve is a decent welcome, wouldn't you say?"
"Hard to deny," admitted Oslac. "Here we find women doing those things normally reserved for the men of the district – and doing it bloody well, too. But then, these are your fellow ship-wives we're talking about: wedded to long periods of coping alone every summer, of bargaining, bartering and buying without anyone else but each other to refer to. Holding the lands, organising the thralls and bondar, keeping everything as it ought to be. Every summer it's happened, for as long as I can remember; but this is the first time any of you have had to pull together and deal with something this serious." He grinned suddenly. "Never mind tales of what your lords have been up to out on the whale's roads: you can tell them a good one in return this year!"
Thordis' mouth twitched. "It's not over yet," she reminded him.

"No," he agreed, "but it's getting there."

The slave sent inside for the ale – Thordis was still having trouble putting names to faces – had shown a spark of inspiration and brought a mate back out with her to hold the other horn. As Asa and Var dismounted with much grumbling and stretching of cramped muscles, Thordis bowed low and with a sweep of her hands sent the thralls forward.

"Welcome," she declared formally, then let the irrepressible grin through once more. "If I ever, ever doubted your friendship towards my lord and I, no doubts could stand in the way of such a splendid and welcome sight!"

"Aye, well, it's a bit different to the usual style of visiting," said Asa with a smile. "You'll know my lord more than you know me just now, but it's not for want of trying to come out to you."

"Lady Asa, you are always welcome here, whatever the chance that brings you! Will you come inside? I have the fire hot and the night-meal stewing... and there is wine, if you care for it..."

"Hard to resist such hospitality, eh, Var?"

Var chuckled. "I've been here already, so I know all about it. Eyvind chose his successors well, I think."

"Hmm; now all we have to do is kick this Onund off your border so you can settle into it properly." Asa shifted her cloak on her shoulders with a shrug and looked around. "Nia? Where are you, lass? Come to me; come on inside, and bring my shoes." She turned her attention back to Thordis. "I take it you'll have folks who can see our lads bedded in?"

"Anlaf said he'd attend to it, so they're in the best of hands. I think he's planning on putting them in all together in the big shed out by Eyvind's mound, so they'll not be alone or with strangers. And then tomorrow, we can march them out and see what Onund wants to make of it." She cast a glance towards Oslac, but the lawman merely raised an eyebrow in silence. "So then," she continued brightly, "come inside, my friends, and let me hear all about everything. If we can put off talk of fighting and bloodshed until another day, so much the better. Hopefully a good show of spears will be sufficient."

"And if it isn't," added Oslac, "we'll find out soon enough."

CHAPTER FORTY-SIX

Thordis lived up to the reputation of Eyvindstoft as
a place of fine feasting and good entertainment: once
the boiled pork and sheep had been served, there was
fresh bread, herring both fresh and barrelled, barley
pottage laced with thyme and onion, and griddlecakes
dripping with butter and honey. Wine stood on
the central table, whilst a succession of serving-men
carried ale around the lower tables of the hall almost
continually. Once the eating had finished, the tables
were cleared away and folk produced pipes, horns
and even a lyre made an appearance; Bjarni the skald
sang poems that most people would know and love
around the weaving-platform, whilst dancers filled the
rest of the floor. The night went on, hot in the glow of
the hearth-flame and full of fun and joy and laughter.
Then came the morning. Misty and chill, it sent an
uncanny echo of their own condition to many of those
stood shivering in the yard, watching water form on
the sharp tips of spears as they waited in the swirls of
thin, clinging fog. The doors of the hall were shut; its
bulk loomed black and indistinct before them as they
munched on remnants of bread and cold meat brought
out by a handful of the housemaids – who looked no
better than the assembled warband after their own
celebrations through the night. One or two found
excuses to linger by certain of the visitors, but never
long enough to warrant too much attention – or
jealousy. There was, after all, a strong chance that not
all of these lads would walk back as whole or hale as
they were about to march outwards, and comfort was
a thing easily given for a little while.
The porch-door slowly creaked open as
Eyvindstoft's own men joined those already waiting.
The three ladies of the ship, along with the
Lawspeaker, stood on the threshold and surveyed
their forces through somewhat bleary, reddened eyes.

"Blame it on the fire," Thordis had advised them as they gathered over a morning cup and a few scraps of fish, "it never rises right in the mornings."

Standing in the shade of the door, Var attempted to count their strength, but the mist defeated her; that and the unwillingness of her own eyes to even focus just yet. "I can't make a tally," she sighed eventually. "My lord, can your eyes do better than mine?"

"Anlaf!" roared Oslac, making his companions wince suddenly. "Have you a tally yet?"

"I make eighty-six, my lord," came the answer as Anlaf strode towards them. He bowed to each in turn before continuing. "We have twenty from Lisceardr, another twenty-three from Brynjolfsburgh, and the thirteen that came with you, my lord. Plus the thirty we mustered among us here... yes, that makes eightysix, doesn't it?" He turned to look back at the huddled mass. "Quite a showing for a district such as this, I'd think... and there's another thirty or so on the ship, of course." He whistled a long, low note. "That's impressive."

"Hopefully also frightening," said Thordis through gritted teeth. "Ingebjorg: go find my bow and its arrows and bring them to me; Osmund, go get the horses for us." She turned back to Anlaf. "Right then: put their captains at the head of each set of men and make them ready to march."

Her overseer grinned and jammed a rusty iron helm over his padded cap. "Well, I'm ready... and it won't take long to sort the others out. With your leave, I'll come back to you when we're set to go."

Oslac raised an eyebrow at Thordis as the man departed. "You are taking a bow, my lady?"

Thordis shrugged. "Where we lived before, on the edges of the Westmorlanders, *everyone* had a bow... I've worn breeks before, too, my lord, when the need arose." She grinned at him. "And I'll do it all again when the need arises, as now. If you're going to get all legal and proprietorial about it, allow me at least to warn you that you're wasting your breath!"

Oslac looked surprised and somehow hurt. "It only becomes my concern, my lady, if your husband ever brings it before the Thing in pursuit of a divorce claim against you... but somehow I don't think that's very likely to happen either. Any man who complained of his wife taking such measures in protection of his lands and property doesn't deserve such loyalty, after all, wouldn't you say? So I'll even offer to string your bow should you wish it – and I have mine in my baggage, although I'll content myself in the first instance with carrying my axe and my sword."

"We brought a handful of bows," put in Var.

"I think we can save worrying about deployments and tactics until they become needful," said Oslac thoughtfully. "Let's not make a skirmish into a war just yet." As their horses ambled into view, he moved forwards to meet them. "The whole point of all this, after all, is to allow Onund the chance to withdraw peaceably, certain of what he goes up against if his disturbances continue. We aren't, or shouldn't be, talking of marching on Hrafnkelsby and smashing it just yet."

"Don't look at me!" protested Asa, "I never said a word!"

"Madam, you have a look," responded the lawman, "that says more than mere words could ever do."

Had it not been for the sounds and subliminal presence of so many armed men walking just behind them, the ride out into Thordis' meadows could have been a chilly pleasure. The mist swirled around the horses' hooves, but bright skies above them gave a promise of it burning away long before the forenoon was up; birds were in the hedgerows and trees, and every once in a while there was a rustling in the undergrowth that spoke of weasels or hares or voles settling in to watch their progress. On the riverwards side, the fields rolled gently downhill towards its shores; the sounds of rhythmic waves slapping on the sand wafted quietly towards them on the faintest of breezes. Var exhaled slowly, feeling tensions within her easing as she did so. They would be back, of course; they could hardly be expected to stay away as she rode at the head of an army, riding with them to possible bloodshed and slaughter. In a sudden moment, she wondered how in all the worlds her husband, Hrolf the shipmaster, son of Dubhnjall the sailor, Dubhnjall the raider and slave-taker, ever coped with the strains of his command. For that one fleeting moment, Var would have given almost anything to not be where she was just then. Responsibility came flooding in upon her; somehow, it felt as if all this had been engineered by her own actions – and now came the consequence and the wyrd from it all. Then Asa swore as her horse stumbled on a rock, and the spell was broken. She wasn't alone, and these actions, these deeds, were not only of her making. Plenty of others had a hand in them as well, Onund not least of all. Let him carry some of the blame, then, she said to herself; better still, let him have it all. She somehow doubted that his own moment of doubt and worry would be as brief as hers.

CHAPTER FORTY-SEVEN

Shabby figures joined them as they walked into the fields: herdsmen of cattle and sheep, whose homes lay out in those same fields, rough shacks and not in the same class at all as the halls of those as mighty in the land as Var and her companions. "I gave instructions for them to move all our own animals away from the meadows," Thordis explained, her words sounding loud and strangely echoing through the mist. "Any that we find from now onwards will have come from Hrafnkelsby, and I intend to keep them for my own."

"Harsh words," observed Asa with interest.

Thordis shrugged.

"Sister, would you do anything else under these circumstances? Perhaps it's just the legacy of where we lived before," she went on reflectively, "in those parts, sheep strayed where they would, regardless of what their masters wanted. So folk would round 'em all up and once a year there'd be a great sorting-out of stock, with gelds paid for any eaten in the meantime. Maybe not an ideal system, but it worked well enough."

"I daresay, but here we're not talking about strays, though."

Thordis raised an eyebrow. "Aren't we? These animals aren't mine, if we find any of course: I've taken pains to make sure of that. So if they're not mine, but they're on my land, what can they be but strays? The only alternative is to say that they were deliberately driven here without my agreement, and that, I'm told, is a clear breach of the local laws. In calling them stray, I'm doing Onund a service he doesn't deserve."

"Remind me never to anger you, lady Thordis," Asa surrendered with a laugh. "And there we were wondering how well you'd cope in this new house and all!"

"The lady Var will tell you how well I was doing earlier this summer," she replied. "If I'm strong and happy in what I'm doing now, it's only through the support of you all. I won't forget that."

Asa waved the compliment aside. "Your lord has a share in the ship, as do ours. Of course we'd stand with you, no matter what the circumstance. As it happens, I can't see that you've put even a foot wrong so far; if we've provided anything, it's only spears and a bit of moral support. We don't see as much of each other as perhaps we ought, by and large – or Var and I don't, anyway. We've usually got enough to occupy us at home, and Gytha's far enough away that she might as well be overseas... but we rally when we need to. Let's face it, if we didn't, then men like Onund would walk roughshod over us, and for all his good intentions Oslac here would like as not ignore us as well, or at least until the ship came home and we could load all our complaints onto our husband's shoulders for presentation at the autumn Thing. But by then, in this instance especially, it would be too late, wouldn't it? I wouldn't mind betting that we've cut it fine enough already."

"In what way?"

"In turning an initial intrusion, and thus an unlawful act, into an established practice and custom," supplied Oslac gravely. "You have it right, lady Asa, although I'm hoping that Onund has less precise knowledge of such matters than you do. Had you left his sheep grazing your lands for, say, a season, lady, then he might have been able to persuade enough men that he had established a traditional right to graze so, to make a case of it at the Thing. And the longer you had left it thereafter, for whatever reason, the stronger his position would have become. It's good to know, however, that Eyvindstoft is in such capable hands; I dream of quiet Things where nothing happens, and with your actions so far that dream is one step closer to coming true."

"So you'll be hosting us all at your booth for the duration, then?" grinned Var wickedly. "Hrolf will be home: better get more ale made!"

Oslac refused to rise to the bait. "It would be worth the expense," he declared with a straight face, "aye, even worth the possible ruin of my household through the drinking-habits of *all* our ship-lords, if I were to be granted the rest and freedom from legal arguments that ought to go with such a price." He sniffed. "I doubt if even the sons of Ingimund could disturb my happiness under those circumstances."

"There," announced Anlaf, who had ridden ahead slightly, and now came back to join them. "There are sheep clustered around the edge of the meadow up ahead, and there are men in with them."

"They'll have heard us even if we've not been seen yet," Oslac added.

"Good," said Thordis, sitting a little more upright in her saddle, "I want us seen. Anlaf: send the word for all the lads to line up across the way here: show them the bulk of our number. Ladies, sisters, my lord Lawspeaker... would you advance alongside me?"

"That ought to make for quite a showing," said Asa. Var nodded, and flicked her reins.

She saw no faces she recognised from Hrafnkelsby, but then she hadn't paid very close attention to the men who had escorted her to the hall there. She wondered briefly if Elle might have done better, but then discounted the idea of having her daughter this close to potential trouble. Those faces at which she peered so intently had wheeled to face their approach; she noticed spears among their number, but also that they fell to their knees in the presence of nobility. Or perhaps it was due to the gradual appearance of more and more armed men advancing towards them over a slight rise in the ground. There were only half-a-dozen or so, in danger of being attacked by over eighty. Bold moves on their part suddenly seemed foolhardy in the extreme.

"I am Thordis, lady of Eyvindstoft," began their hostess. "The lands on which you are grazing your animals are mine under law. I have witnesses and tokens to that effect, so you are guilty of trespass on these lands, and who knows what else besides. Now give me a reason why I shouldn't just have you hanged for your offences against me." That was all she said: nothing more seemed to be required. The men looked at each other; uncertainty vied with fear, but also with arrogant bravado.

"Lady," one said eventually, "we have none among us who is our leader: we are just shepherds. We follow our flock where we must..."

"There is no demand on you that you follow them – or send them – onto *my* lands!" exploded Thordis. "Someone put you up to this, and I will have his name; otherwise, my men here will have you strung up by nightfall, and your sheep can go into the stew along with mine. Anlaf: my bow." She held out a hand imperiously; the overseer handed over the weapon without comment, and then supplied the arrow to match it. Here and there among the rank of men behind her, the sounds of stringing bows could also be heard.

"Did your lord instruct you to do this?" asked Thordis, her voice sounding like iron. She drew back the string, and sighted along the shaft. "Did he even so much as *suggest* that you trespass on my lands?"

"Lady, for pity's sake, stay!" cried one of the grovelling men. "Let us at least answer before you put shafts in us all... the tale is complex and not at all clear, even to me."

"It ought to be clear," commented Oslac. "Do you know who I am?"

"You are the lord Lawspeaker, sir," came the reply. "I was with my master when he spoke with you at the

Thing."

"Then you ought to be aware of the danger you are in from us all," continued Oslac. "I ride alongside these ladies: what does that tell you?"

There was a slump of shoulders as realisation began to sink in. "It tells me that we are outwith the law in this," the man said slowly. "Very well sir, I will tell you what you need to know. Just please, lady, hear us out before you decide on our fate: we aren't bad men. We have families, and rent to pay..."

"I don't care for any of that," retorted Thordis. "Those things are your problems, not mine. Now speak up, and stop wasting my day."

"She's harsh," whispered Asa, sounding somewhat awestruck.

"Makes you glad you took the time to be a friend, eh?" answered Var. Her companion nodded silently, fascination on her features.

"We are bonded men under Onund of Hrafnkelsby," began the closest of the huddled men, wiping his face with one hand and being careful to keep both in plain sight. "Before he came, we were tenants of Hadding Ulfheresson; most of us came out of Mercia with him when the old king granted him this estate."

"That puts many of them back before our people's coming," murmured Oslac to those around him.

"We had no need to look far for grazing until Onund came to be lord over us," their informant continued sadly. "But since his coming, things have got worse and worse. Now the fields around the hall go unmanaged – he won't allow us in them, says he has grander plans for the land there. But much of the commonland is inaccessible, with little in the way of feed for man or beast; when some of us put all this to the lord, he suggested we look farther out if we were dissatisfied with his provision. But sir, lady, he doesn't provide for us at all! Grain and meat and flour come in from time to time, aye, but it all goes to the hall; we get nothing. We scratch our livings from little patches around our houses where we can grow roots and leaves and keep our hens; but we have our stock as well, and they need to graze. We were driven out of our usual lands, lady, because their condition is such that we can get no useful grazing from them."

"But you saw fit to just come over the boundary and not inform anyone, or ask their leave," Oslac pointed out, forestalling Thordis' own answer. "It is that which puts you outside the law, man, and there are no conditions which might alter that."

There was a trace of a bleak grin. "I would not presume to argue law with you, lord. Lady, we are in your hands. We have nothing to offer in compensation to you but our own lives; but if you decide to hang us for this, who will carry word to our wives and children? Whose protection could they call upon? Onund's demands are harsh enough sometimes; for all that he expects little from us in the way of service to him, there is the yearly scat, and the rents, and his food-dues all to pay..."

Thordis had lowered her bow during this talking; now she quietly removed the arrow from the string. "You'll not hang," she said, although there was still hardness in her tone, and it was clear that nothing had been forgiven. "Lord Oslac, is there a message that these wretches could take back to their master for you? I have one for them to spread around their bench-mates: don't come back here. The next intruders *will* be dead, either by rope or bow or spear." She leaned forwards on her horse slightly. "Make sure all your friends hear that, and make sure they understand. As it is, your animals are forfeit: they are on my lands, so I claim them as mine. Now get back to your homes, and be thankful for my generosity."

"Wait," said Oslac as they prepared to scurry away.

"How much of what you do does your master know about? How will he take the loss of these sheep?"
"He never directly told us to do this, lord, but I think he must have worked it out by now," came another voice, from a thin, rat-faced man with a straggly moustache after the Mercian style. "As to how he will respond to your intervention, I really wouldn't know, sir. Sometimes he takes an interest, but more often he doesn't. He's away a lot of the time, and we don't see the lady his mother at all."
Out of sight, Var nodded quietly to herself. "Where does he go, your master?" asked Oslac.
"We don't know, lord: he never bothers with the likes of us. But if it helps at all, he travels out on the easterly road more than any other, as if he were heading back into Mercian holdings."
"Had any visitors come by lately?"
"A fine-looking man with a handful of well equipped mates," came the reply. "Less than a se'ennight ago, I think. I saw them arriving but I didn't mark when they left."
"Alright, I think that will do. Go; and be thankful for the good spirit of the lady here. And remember her warning!"
"So," breathed Thordis after the men had shambled out of sight, "I have caused this gathering of forces for nothing after all."
"Don't be so sure," advised Oslac. "Lady, I think it would be wise to keep these spears close by for a short while yet: I'm not at all sure that this business is fully done with."
"That news of a well-dressed visitor at Hrafnkelsby is bothering you?" asked Var.
"Indeed, lady. There might be nothing in it, of course, but such folk putting in an appearance at just this time has the smell of more than coincidence to it." He retreated into thought for a moment or two, his breath steaming and mingling with that of his pony. "I

ought to go to Hrafnkelsby," he decided, "and I ought to go now. I can use today's incidents as a pretext: it could be considered in my interest to be sure that Onund knows the full story and gives pledges to control his men better, in order to avoid any escalations. If I do that, then we remain fully within the law and the customs of these lands, and whatever he does next places him just as firmly outside that law as his shepherds were."

"You speak as if convinced that he is going to do more," said Var slowly. "But from what I saw of him, I would've thought any action to be unlikely. Too much effort."

"But I suspect he is not alone in this any more: he has another pushing him onwards now. He's had his gifts, and now it's repayment time for them: he will have to act if my suspicions are true, or lose everything he's tried to build. So if you would, my ladies, don't take your men home for a few days yet. Not until I get back from this errand, at any rate. Then I should have more news."

"When do you plan to leave?" asked Asa.

"I'll take six of my men and go right now," answered the lawman. "Hrafnkelsby's the shortest of rides from here, and this ought not to take any real length of time."

So saying, he pulled his horse's head up from the grass, and wheeled back towards the knot of spears behind them. The three ship-women watched him go in silence.

"Well," said Thordis after a lengthy pause. "I suppose there's still the hall to prepare, food to organise for these men, cloth to weave..."

"I wish you better luck than I've had with my loom," snorted Var. "Every time I go near it, something happens and I have to come away again."

"Good to see that you can still smile about it, though," observed Asa. She turned to Thordis once more. "If he hadn't answered, would you really have shot him?"

"Oh yes," she answered brightly. "I learned at an early age that you never threaten something like that unless you intend going through with it."

"That sounds like it must have been a hard lesson." Clouds covered Thordis' eyes for a moment.

"Aye," she said more quietly, "that it was. But folk say that it's usually the hardest knocks that you tend to remember. Hopefully those idiots had enough of a knock today to hold them back in future. And I have more sheep! Won't Einar be pleased?"

"Lady, you have a sense of humour that would put the trolls to shame!" Asa shuddered slightly. "Still, as you say, there's been some good had out of all this. Although I'm not sure I like the way our Lawspeaker's mind is turning."

They brought their ponies round and walked them slowly back towards their fidgeting, restless men. "No fighting for today, lads," called out Asa as they passed.

"Back to the house, then, lady?" enquired Anlaf. Thordis nodded. "Leave, oh, a dozen or so behind us here, though, and arrange for food and ale to be brought out to them. I want a watch kept over these fields for a bit – at least until the lord Oslac returns. The rest of these can take their turns at it... did we really put eighty-odd men into the field today? Gods, that would count as a proper army in some places! How did that happen?"

"There might well be more tomorrow," said Var unexpectedly. Her companions turned in their saddles to look at her.

"Word spreads," she reminded them. "Even though Onund's men go straight back to him and talk to no other, even though Oslac's escort have no chance to gossip anywhere, and even though we keep these lads at Eyvindstoft and none of us go home just yet, by tomorrow morning, folk will know what's happened here. Don't ask me how: it just happens. So don't be too surprised if more spears start trickling in over the day to swell your ranks; and don't be too upset when some of them go Onund's way, either. If Oslac is right in his thinking that Onund has got in with Ingolf, there are some who'll see their best chance on that side of the ditch, be it lawful or no." She swept her gaze across the long line of spears. "But unless he can get Ingolf to bring his own *hird* in on his side, Onund won't be able to match our numbers. Hold tight sister," she advised grimly, "as the lawman said, this isn't over just yet."

CHAPTER FORTY-EIGHT

Oslac returned to Eyvindstoft sooner than even he had expected: late in that same day, his horn was heard in the outfields and shortly thereafter he and his companions could be seen riding in good order towards the cluster of buildings that made up the steading.
"You must be wearing grooves in that door-sill this summer," smiled Var as once more Thordis stood at her threshold to welcome her visitor.
"I reckon someone'll owe me a new pair of shoes for it," she agreed. "And I ought to put some folk to the brewing, too. We seem to drink as much outdoors as in, these days, with all these comings and goings." She gnawed her lower lip as her eyes remained fixed on Oslac's approach. "I wonder what he found out that brought him back so swiftly? Maybe the men will see some spear-play after all."
"You looking to turn into a valkyrie after you die?" wondered Asa. "For my own part, I'm nowhere near as keen to see blood shed as you appear to be."
"A different upbringing perhaps?" wondered Thordis. "It's not that I'm encouraging it, really I'm not... but I've seen how these things have a habit of ending in nastiness, no matter how hard we try to avoid it. I sometimes wonder if it might be better just to get it over with, nice and quickly. That's all... " Her voice tailed off as the Lawspeaker rode through the gateway marking the hall-yard; at their mistress' signal, men ran forward to take reins and lead the horses away as soon as their riders had climbed off.
"My ladies," Oslac bowed. Thordis returned the gesture, the horn held out before her. "Be welcome once again, my lord."
Oslac sipped and passed the vessel to his companions; once they had all drunk, Thordis was able to formally invite them into the hall. There they

washed faces and hands before moving to seats placed along a table at the side of the hearth. Thordis took the High Seat; Asa and Var took now-familiar places to either side, whilst Anlaf perched on the end of a bench to listen.

"So then: what news?" Thordis could hardly contain her anxiety. "I hadn't expected you back so soon: is aught wrong? Is there anything we ought to be doing?"

"My lady, there is no need for fear or worry," Oslac soothed. "I went to Hrafnkelsby, as you know, in order to present the facts of this matter to Onund and judge his reaction. But I was also interested in his response toward his recent sponsor, and in that I wasn't disappointed."

"Why?" asked Var, leaning forward into the firelight. "What did he do?"

"He merely turned to his left and asked what our lord Ingolf advised."

"Ah," said Asa sagely, "so he *was* there then!"

"And in the High Seat," amended Oslac, "which is something that tells us a great deal by itself. Onund left the entire matter up to his judgement..."

"Sounds about right," sniffed Var disdainfully. "Get out of any work no matter what the cost."

"... but also in effect admitted that he had known about this action of his bondsmen," continued the Lawspeaker, ignoring the interruption.

"But that means," said Thordis slowly, "that we are now having to deal with Ingolf instead. That's not so good, surely? He's not going to be frightened by our makeshift *hird* – or even by your authority, my lord. What did Ingolf decide? Does he settle, or does he fight over this?"

"That remains to be seen," replied Oslac. "He asked me to say that he will visit in a day or two, with a view to conducting negotiations directly."

Var whistled. "Well there's a thing!" she exclaimed

wide-eyed. "I don't recall either of Ingimund's sons ever stirring themselves in our direction before... mind you, part of that might've been down to Hrolf and the others taking great pains to avoid getting them interested."

"Oh dear," said Thordis worriedly. "That doesn't sound so good. Is this going to upset things for you? It wasn't the intention, truly it wasn't!"

"Hush," Asa reassured her. "How is it that the fierce creature we saw earlier becomes such a frightened child within her own hall? Now don't fret so," she went on, patting Thordis on the hand as she might a kitten or an upset child, "what's done is done and there's nothing can alter it. If Ingolf chooses to come here, we can't do anything to stop him short of declaring an outbreak of disease! And even then he might come anyway; but it's true enough that we don't see a great deal of them in these parts, even though it's their *odal* lands from here to the ocean. And yes it's also true that we've all done our best to lie low and just pay our rents and scats when asked, on the basis that having those two involved in our business was likely to get difficult for everyone. It's no secret that they're in two minds regarding the ship and what it does: sometimes they're happy to take the dues we send from it, and other times they seem to want it finished with... although I also reckon there are times when they want it for themselves," she added darkly. "I can't speak for Hrolf but I know Eyvind fought a long campaign with their fathir to keep the ship out of his hands."

"There've been rumblings and, shall we say, *enquiries* from time to time," Var confirmed. "The ship-business is risky enough as it is, but were it to fall into other hands I'd be seriously worried for their safety. We use the ship as a means to better our livelihoods," she explained to Thordis' increasingly blank looks. "The men go out every summer and they come back with goods, silver, sometimes thralls and other things that we either keep or sell on closer to home – usually to the Mercians. And that's it: it's ours, we benefit from it, and we take the risks that go with it. This is how it's always been, all through times past, even before our people came out of their old homes in the North Way. But Ingimund, and now his sons... they view it differently. They're nobility, proper nobility, with lots of lands, rents, titles and all that. To them, the ship would just be another aspect of their *hird*, to be called on whenever they needed transport over sea, or needed to impress someone with what they owned, or felt the need to go plundering to fill their own coffers. An entirely different proposition, and one that holds no profits for the men crewing it – or their families."

"I see," said Thordis quietly. "What do we do if I *have* put this arrangement in danger? What answer do we give to Ingolf if his price for enforcing Onund's compliance is access to the ship? It's hard to imagine, from what you've said, that he's really coming here to bargain for a fair solution: his sort don't have the need for that." She chewed a fingernail distractedly. "At least he's given me time enough to straighten this place out a bit before he arrives... but what's he really coming here for?"

"More importantly," suggested Asa, "if he starts demanding what we don't wish to give, how do we say no and still walk away?"

CHAPTER FORTY-NINE

Ingolf was every inch the chieftan: from his carefully cut and combed reddish-blonde hair, styled low over his forehead and ending in a neat line around the back of his head just above his ears, to his clean and immaculately-cut shoes, made in the newest of styles with a wrapover top-part that secured with a toggle just above the instep and worn over both white linen hose and woollen socks in a vibrant bright blue, he exuded wealth, power and authority. His *kyrtle* was of bright red wool, finely woven and decorated with complicated patterns of braid at neck and cuffs; beneath it could be seen flashes of a blue linen shirt, which Var thought excessive in the height of the summer even as she admired the statement it was there to make. As he entered the hall at Eyvindstoft, Ingolf pulled his travelling cloak over his head – which revealed its more expensive herringbone-twill lining – and tossed it casually to one of his attendants. He pointedly did not remove his sword, whose inlaid iron hilt glittered in the firelight. The women looked at each other quietly; Var and Thordis both managed to shoot more furtive glances towards Oslac, but got nothing in return.

"So then," Ingolf began, settling himself in the High Seat and gesturing for his companions to scatter around the room. Thordis sat herself in her traditional place to the right of the pillars; Oslac helped himself to the other side. After a moment's confusion, Var frowned slightly and laid claim to the table right before the hearth, putting herself directly before their guest, and gestured for Asa to join her.

"So," Ingolf said again. "This is all about the doings of Onund, master of Hrafnkelsby – or rather, the doings of his bondar, for there is no evidence that Onund himself has been involved in any of this."

"Your pardon lord," said Thordis, standing again to

pour ale as a jug arrived, "but that's not entirely so. The men we waylaid a day or so back gave a very clear indication that their master knew – or at least could guess – what they were up to. Whilst admitting that it's not enough to begin a legal case on, it's more than nothing, too."

"You have to accept that their word would not be worth very much before the district judges," replied Ingolf with a touch of indulgent patience in his voice, "whereas Onund knows how to conduct himself in such company. He would swear all the appropriate oaths to declare his innocence, and while his neighbours might think him a fool for not controlling his people better, they would be unwilling, I think, to take matters any further than that." He sipped his ale appreciatively. "I have persuaded him of this already: he is prepared to do it, should it become necessary, since he is in my debt already somewhat." Bright green eyes glittered over the rim of the horn he held. "Would such an ending be acceptable, lady?"

"Lord," Thordis said carefully, "my only concern is that I have no further intrusions onto my lands. If, as seems possible, your man Onund has decided that some of my estate here ought rightfully to be his, then declaring himself innocent of trespass *in this instance* does not seem to address the main issue. So I fear that, as it stands, I would have to decline your offer, sir. And I am sorry to have to do it, but my own duty is clear: I stand guard over these lands we inherited, my husband and I, all according to law and custom, until my husband returns home and can take this up with Onund directly."

The air palpably chilled. Ingolf took another long drink, his eyes hooded. Across the table from her as they were, Var and Asa found themselves out of reach to even squeeze a hand in support. All they could do was watch, and listen, and try to work out where Ingolf's real motives lay.

"Not easy, dealing with men at this level, is it?" murmured Asa in Var's ear, mirroring a movement of Ingolf's as he turned to speak with Oslac. "We're out of our depth here; I just hope Thordis is feeling as confident as she's looking."

"It would be good to think so," came the reply, equally quietly, "but the truth is that whenever it gets this high, who do we turn to? Husbands and landlords, that's who. Oh, we can speak up at the Thing if we really have a need to, and the Gods can help any who cross us in our own halls... but this sort of business ought to be for the men. I can't read him at all; I've got no clues to go by. If Thordis has to end up threatening fights and rebellion, my fear is that we'd have to go through with it."

"Mm, there's no backing down at this level, and no way for us to stop it getting that far – or not that I can see. At this point, I think we have to rely on Oslac."

"Aye... but he's Ingolf's man as well as our Lawspeaker..."

"Oslac tells me," Ingolf suddenly resumed, "that since nobody has any proof of Onund's involvement – and that word 'proof' is important here – all that can result from taking any action against him is a stalemate. Much as I might want to propose such a solution, even I can see that it won't achieve anything: nothing would be settled. Now, from my conversations with Onund, I understand that he regards the portions of meadow running along the old hedge as having once been attached to his estate; somehow, at some point in the past, they became detached, and then became part of this holding. That is the basis for his claim to them; and I have to warn you that he is prepared to push that claim, and not only before the Thing. If it does come to action of any sort, I would be honour-bound to offer him my support. And," he added, idly stroking his sword-hilt, "that is not a minor consideration."

"Nevertheless, sir," retorted Thordis coldly, "my own companions and I put eighty-odd spears in those meadows only a day or so back: I'm surprised Onund didn't mention it, since I'm pretty sure it's a lot more than he could muster without imposing on your own goodwill. Those men and their weapons are still here; it's a simple matter to put them back in the fields and test this man's resolve. Did he by any chance say when he thought these meadows had allegedly changed hands, sir? It would help a great deal in solving this problem if we could find men who remembered it happening, wouldn't you say?"

"Whenever he claims it was," said Oslac drily, "it is doubtful if you will discover any witnesses, lady. For I am certain it hasn't happened since I came here as Lawman: but I have the tokens and such at home, and I will make sure. Lord," he went on, turning to Ingolf, "I ought to warn you as a loyal man that Onund may well be selling you a bad bargain here. Whatever he's basing this claim on is beginning to sound highly suspect, and if he questions my integrity or competence, then I will have to stand against him, however much you might wish to keep his favour by indulging him in this."

"Oh, so it's an indulgence, is it?" growled the lord. "Onund has been useful with his contacts to the Mercians, and at a time when my brother and I agree that closeness to the new king is the best policy to keep us all safe and unharmed, such things command high prices. Lady, what actual difference will the loss of these meadows to Onund make to your own household? What if I were to offer something in return for them: in effect, what if I buy them from you? Would you object if I then chose to give them to Onund?" He spread his hands wide. "From what I saw on my way here, you aren't short of grazing, or of growing-soil. Might that not be an answer?"

"We have not been in this place for very long, sir,"

said Thordis, "and so it might be that we haven't yet discovered the value or worth to us of these lands that Onund claims are his. But what I do know is that he never seems to have made any sort of claim on them while my husband's uncle, Eyvind, was living here and building the place up. I do have to wonder why he chooses this time, especially when my husband is away on-ship, to make such a claim, when he must realise that it cannot be properly answered until Einar's return, and then would surely have to go before the Thing..."

"If I offer silver for the land, it is no business of the Thing," Ingolf pointed out. "It could all be done and finished by the time your ship comes home, and brings all your husbands back to you." He nodded towards Var and Asa.

"You say, sir, that Onund's friendship rates highly with you just now," said Var, taking the plunge and catching the lord's eye. "I'm assuming from this, that you know he's been proposing other deals over this summer?"

Ingolf smiled warily. "He mentioned that he had been to see you at Lisceardr, lady, aye."

"So might I ask if I can expect you at my doorstep as you have come to my lady Thordis, to press Onund's case for him?"

The green eyes glittered again. "You make me sound as if I were a common messenger, lady."

"Never that, sir. The quality of the visitor is the thing that tends to make the impression."

"Well then, let me ask how you would answer any such visit?"

"As I told master Onund, sir, such matters as my daughter's marriage would have to be discussed with my husband on his return," said Var archly. "After all, it's not something that could be finalised with a promise of good silver, now is it?"

Ingolf smiled a bit more warmly. "No, lady, I

would have to say it wasn't – or shouldn't be. I have two daughters of my own, and so I can easily appreciate your position. But I came here to sound out the lady Thordis, and that ought to be where my business lies, at least for today. Lady, would you at least consider my offer? I am guesting with Onund for the usual three nights, so I can offer you another day to think on it. My lord Oslac, I give you the necessary freedoms to advise rightly and properly in this, should you be asked. I ought to be making my way back to Hrafnkelsby, and keeping an eye on my host." He grinned at the women suddenly. "I think I've got enough to do without him deciding to take matters into his own hands as well!"

CHAPTER FIFTY

Oslac left shortly after Ingolf, riding furiously in the other direction, heading for Thorsteinn's tun and home in order to check his memory and that of the whole district as it was recorded on tallies and tokens. These kept the details of every land sale, every legal action, every property dispute ever aired within the *herred*, and so they also held the key to the matter of who owned the hedgerow meadows between Hrafnkelsby and Eyvindstoft. In his absence, the shipwomen attended to the looms, peered into kettles, and wondered where the next surprise would be coming from.

"I'm both fascinated and worried by Ingolf's getting so close in with Onund," admitted Var as she wound yet more wool into balls from its frame. "After what his wife told us, I can't see how he's possibly managed to keep our lord fooled for so long – or so well."

"Well, he's got his mothir there to help him," Thordis pointed out. "And he doesn't have Elfgyfu there to argue against him, either. She went back to her own folk in Mercia, did I tell you? She hoped that maybe the wind had changed, and she might get at least a hearing from them. I sent a messenger along with her to add our weight to her case and I hope it works in her favour: she deserves some good luck out of all this. But going back to Onund, what with your own comments about how he keeps apart from his bondsmen, I can imagine it would be very easy to be fooled – especially if you were going there without any definite motive against him."

"Aye, but that's only going to last for so long, ain't it?" said Asa dismissively. "You can't keep folk in the dark forever – and say what else you like about him, Ingolf's not an idiot. He's got his own men around him, and they're going to be feeding their own findings back to him... if we can just get Oslac to come right out and say that those lands are, and always have been, yours, then I think this business ought to be finished."

"Leaving him free to try again for Elle," murmured Var darkly. "That sympathetic-yet-elusive answer I got from Ingolf worries me."

"Don't fret so," retorted Asa. "He's hardly likely to just abduct her, now is he? Not even Ingolf would stand aside for such behaviour, much less collude in it. The summer marches on: every day is one closer to the men getting back and bringing their own experience and war-skill, should we need it. That's one thing in our favour: the longer we draw this out, the stronger we get. Onund wants it finished before then, because if he's unable to sway us then he's got no chance against the *felag-menn*."

"And yet the pressure to settle is getting stronger," Var pointed out. "What started as a little squabble between bondsmen is now involving the lord of the district, the Lawspeaker and three households. Four, if you count Hrafnkelsby... and this is only one of two questions been raised this summer." She looked around at her companions. "Sisters, we have to do *something...*"

"There's little we can do," admitted Thordis wearily. "I'm supposed to be considering Ingolf's offer: it's generous enough, and if we asked Oslac to set the price, I'm sure it would be a fair one. But I don't want to do that: we were given this place, as it stood, barely a season ago, and I'm loath to let any of it go. I don't trust Onund, and if Oslac comes back to us confirming that this land has never been divided or sold or whatever, then I'd rather stand firm and see both Onund and his master off. But I'm also mindful of the consequences that might arise from doing that; life could get awkward for us all as time goes on. I'm sure Ingolf and his brother could bring all sorts of unpleasant pressures to bear, should they choose to."

"It's been good not having them opposing us," agreed Asa, "but Brynjolf has often said that it's only a matter of chance, and that whenever they decide they want something from us, that indifference would change." She smiled bleakly. "Seems he was right, don't it?"

"Between us, we have eighty spears," Thordis urged, although possibly she said it more to herself than to her companions. "Even if Oslac were to take his lads home with him, which he hasn't, we'd still have over sixty. How can that not be enough to send Onund packing? What more could it possibly take?"

"Today might be the day we find out," called Anlaf from the doorway. "Onund's boys are back in the meadows. Lady, what are your commands?"

Thordis rose from her stool by the loom; in the bright lights of the lamps and candles, she suddenly looked inhumanly like one of the Hooded One's gatherers of the slain: thin-faced, bright-eyed, eager for the fight and its harvest of corpses. "Gather our spears," she said clearly and crsiply. "It's time to end this, and screw Ingolf and his silver. Onund knows he's got it wrong; now he's just trying to push his way in."

"Make a show of it and frighten us off?" wondered Asa. Thordis smiled, but there was no humour or warmth to be found in it.

"He hasn't met me before. I don't frighten."

"You scare the bloody hell out of me," muttered Asa. "I'd rather face up against Onund, or even Ingolf, than get on your wrong side."

Thordis beamed. "But we're friends, aren't we? Why should I ever get angry at you? But just think what mention of our friendship might do to anyone who's ever foolish enough to annoy you!"

"Like it or not," agreed Var, "we're becoming as much of a force in this land as our husbands are."

"And we're here all year long," added Thordis. She

leant over and put her spindle down in its basket of raw, unspun fleece. "Come then, sisters: let's stand in our proper place. I'll not send men out to die for me without being there to lead them."

Asa paled. "You're not suggesting we actually take weapons and *fight??"*

"No! Of course not! If I've done it in the past, it's only because there was no choice and nobody else to do it for me. Besides, we were a great deal more insignificant than we are here; couldn't do such things here, not for anything. Decent folk would notice; gossip spreads just as fast as the shit that goes on the fields. No, sister, you have my word that I'll sit my horse and goad our lads onwards as is right and proper for ladies of quality... mind you, if we have miscalculated and Onund gets through us, should we take arms and defend ourselves at the very last?"

"I'll put a dozen or so of the best lads around you, lady," suggested Anlaf, also plainly uneasy at the turns within this latest exchange. "Will you take your bow?"

"I did it last time: aye, I think I should." Thordis grinned suddenly. "Then we have a defence all of our own!"

CHAPTER FIFTY-ONE

There were more men facing them this time: better men too, not just Onund's own scabby, malnourished peasants, who stood off to one side slightly and grasped their motley array of farm implements, bent spears, poor bows and notched, blunted axes from the woodpiles. The rest – Anlaf did a quick count and reckoned they made another thirty or so – were a great deal better, in their appearance and their equipment. There was actually a dim shine of iron from their spear-points as they caught the fitful, clouded sunlight; that same shine illuminated a handful of iron helmets as well as shield-rims. There was no mist to hide them today; Thordis and her house-guests rode to the fore of their own men, hastily gathered from sheds and barns and even the fields, where they had been usefully filling their time as they awaited the call to go home.

"We still outnumber them, then," murmured Thordis as her overseer reported back to her. "Unless someone – and it has to be Ingolf, to judge from what you say about the quality of these new men – has held more back out of sight, there's little to stop us just charging them and knocking them all over, surely." She bit her lower lip, deep in thought. "It's a big chance to take... but..."

"Send out a few of our nimbler lads," suggested Var. "Send 'em out wide and out-of-sight; tell 'em to try and get around behind that line of men. If they find aught, then they can come back and tell us; if we keep maybe a third of ours here and away from prying eyes, then it'll look as if we're more evenly matched and hopefully Ingolf won't think the way you just did. If he throws all of his lads straight in, then we hold our third back until we see if we need them – and until we learn if there are more on his side waiting, too. It gives us a chance to see what our opponent does... speaking of which, is there any sign of him? We ought to see if he's willing to explain himself, at least."

Anlaf wheeled his pony and headed back towards their presumed foes. "I can't see anyone in front of them," murmured Asa, shielding her eyes. "But it's bright out here: I'm having trouble seeing anything."

Var laughed. "Just as well we let Thordis have the bow, then!"

"There," said Thordis suddenly, pointing. "He's just come out of the line. Or rather, *they* have."

"Oh," said a surprised Var. "Onund actually came out with him?"

"So it would seem," replied Anlaf. "Lady, would you go forward?"

"We all will," she decided firmly. "If Ingolf can drag Onund along with him, then I can take some support as well, can't I? Anlaf, I'll need you with us; find someone to skive off around a third of our lads and keep them back out of sight. Then send those we know can run when they need to: as Var just said, they need to go right around and look for more of Ingolf's men hidden like we've just done with ours. Whatever they find, we need to know as soon as can be."

"Who among you heard that?" called Anlaf. A chorus of responses came back to him. "Then you know what's needed. Sort it out among yourselves - but do it swiftly and quietly, y'hear? Take a third of each hall's lads, the ones at the backs of the marching lines. Come on now, move!"

Men shuffled and jostled to obey; Var was pleased to see Sigurd, her own headman, taking charge of his mates and neighbours and ensuring that things were done correctly. Bad, though, that they had been driven into this, she also thought; but such was life, even for farming bondsmen and the like. There were no promises in this world; safety was a relative thing, after all. It was very probable that, even standing up to face what looked like seasoned, experienced fighting-men in the pay of the local overlord, they might still be safer than if they were out on the ship with Hrolf. She turned back to where Asa was gesturing for her to clear the path and head over to the side; the visible portion of their forces tramped forward as she did so, and then came to a halt just on a slight ridge running across the slope. When she craned her neck to look behind them, the rest of their forces had vanished into the hedgerow and bushes around it.

"Var!" called Asa again. "Come on: Thordis is going forwards!"

She kicked the flanks of her pony and effortlessly caught up. Ahead, a small knot of men detatched themselves from the rest of their troop and strode towards the women.

"You know who's who?" asked Var. Thordis shook her head.

"Well, you've met Ingolf, so he stands out already. The pale-haired one beside him is Onund; and the other two, I don't know either. I don't remember them at Hrafnkelsby, so I'm assuming they're part of Ingolf's crew."

"It's Onund that I'm most interested in," came the reply. "My fingers are itching just to put a shaft to the bow and be done with all this."

"Whatever Einar thinks of your actions so far, sister, I'm not so sure that he'd thank you for leaving him a weregeld to pay over the winter."

"Got any better suggestions?"

"Wait until we're actually fighting: then the rules change."

"Hmm: that's actually better advice than I'd looked for!"

Their talk ceased as their opponents drew closer. Ingolf presented a far more favourable aspect than did

Onund. The lord of Wirhalh had removed his iron helm, and looked comfortable in his mailshirt; by contrast, Onund kept his own headgear firmly in place, and was clearly feeling the weight of the iron on him. Somehow, his wargear seemed not to fit so well; the helmet's rim lay low over his eyes, and was tall enough to look unbalanced on his round, soft features. Similarly, the mail was baggy under the arms, yet tight across the midriff; his shoulders slumped within it, and the belt looked awkward, as if the sword hung from it was dragging the whole thing to one side. Sweat was glistening on Onund's face, and trickling into that pale, almost white beard; not surprisingly from Var's point of view, it was Ingolf who stepped a further pace and began the speaking.

"My ladies," he bowed, without a trace of sarcasm or condescension towards them. "I offer my apologies for moving this business forwards before you had even had a chance to reply to my offer of yesterday; but I was... *persuaded*... that such an answer was likely to be unfavourable. In truth, I set some of my own people to look into Onund's claim, in order to have independent opinion to our lord Oslac's; but I suspect that they will find the same thing. You were right, my lady: there does not appear to be any record or memory of this land ever not being a part of your estate – and your own inheritance of it was witnessed by enough folk at the summer Thing that arguing the point would be ridiculous."

"More ridiculous than bringing armed men here to fight over it anyway?" replied Thordis with her brightest, most engaging smile. "I fear I must be foolish as well, then, since I've done exactly the same!"

"You are most gracious, lady: but for my part, I am driven here by debts of honour and friendship, and however much I might know the basis for my being here to be untrue, still I am duty-bound to come and enter into the sword-play... although I will be happy enough to withdraw as soon as I feel my debt is discharged." He shot a meaningful glance at the sweaty man beside him. Onund merely glowered at the women.

"I thought I had a good claim to this strip," he grumbled, "and I still see no reason why you have to be awkward about letting me have it. It's not as if you need it: my lads report that your animals are very rarely up this way, and beyond a few holes through the hedges, we've done no damage. Instead, though, we're all here with spears and the talk is of fights and blood and such... if you'd just been happy to give a little, lady, we could all have avoided this and gone on much as before."

"And what would you have taken a fancy to once you'd got this meadow?" asked Thordis sweetly. "Might you not have thought that my very hall and my infield were a shade better than your own, and that you ought to have those too? I know your sort, Onund of Mercia: I've met you before, in other folk, up among the Westmorlanders and the Galwaeg. You're never satisfied until you have it all: but you won't work honestly for any of it, and you invent reasons and heritages for yourselves to try and justify your greed. I will not yield a single inch to you, and especially not just because you have the cheek to say I ought to. Were you any sort of man, you'd've waited to take this up with my husband – but I know the answer you'd've got from him, too, and it's not so different from the one you'll have today. You've shown yourself, Onund of Mercia: you showed yourself at Lisceardr, too, doing something similar to my sister here's own daughter! Were you thinking of asking our lord Ingolf to ride with you to Walea and lay siege to the hall there, in order to win another bride? Oh, and the lady Elfgyfu said to remind you that she has no intent of freeing you from the

marriage-vows you made to her and her kin, either."
From the way Ingolf's eyebrows shot up, it was
clear that there was one shaft that had hit its mark.
Thordis smirked slightly, and visibly turned her
attention back to the son of Ingimund.
"So my lord, how is it to be? I have no objection to
my lads having a little play at love-taps with yours, if
you have a mind for the exercise; your friend here
looks as if he could do with it. Were you good
enough to lend him his armour, too?" She sighed
theatrically. "If only our own menfolk were home,
eh? Then it would be better sport for everyone, I'm
thinking: your lads look very capable, but then ours
might perhaps have rather more to actually fight
for..."
"I am not immune to your taunts and insults,
woman," snapped Onund suddenly. "It's not for
nothing that women are known as the inciters of war
and the goads that drive men to awful deeds
sometimes. I put my case: I still think that I've
nothing to be ashamed of. But if you want hard
knocks and the deaths of your best men, then you can
have them."
"Happy with that, lord?" Thordis asked Ingolf.
"It would seem there is little choice left," came the
reply. "Be assured of my friendship in future, and
hopefully more peaceable, times, lady." He bowed
and turned back to his men. Onund merely glared at
his opponents and then followed.
"What a horrid man," commented Asa drily. "No
sense of politeness or good manners at all!"
"It's what comes of being a low-born who dreams
of Jarldoms," replied Var. "Either you learn to control
such tendencies and live with things as they really are
– or you don't, and your delusions end up destroying
you. I suppose that all the time he sat in his own hall,
with nobody but his mother for company, it made no
difference how he was; but I'm surprised that

someone of Ingolf's stature has put up with him at all." She looked at his retreating back thoughtfully. "I'd love to know what he's promised in return for all this; but then I'd love to know how he plans on keeping that promise, too."

"Well, if what Elfgyfu implied is actually the truth, then perhaps one reason for trying his luck with your Elle was to make some useful contacts in the first place," suggested Asa.

Thordis shuddered. "She seemed far too nice a lass for that; we ought to be getting rid of Onund just to keep everyone's daughters safe."

"Lady," interrupted Anlaf, "I'm going to suggest that you move aside now. They're nearly back to their own lads: it won't be long before we have arrows and spears flying all through here."

Var looked around her. "Where do you suggest?" she asked with raised eyebrows. "Short of going back to the hall, I can't see that anywhere in this area is going to be any safer than where we are now."

Anlaf sighed under his breath. "Lady, at least do me the favour of watching from *behind* our own line?"

"I take it you'll be staying here," stated Thordis. Anlaf grinned from under his iron eyebrows and waved an axe playfully.

"Well just make sure you've got your shield as well," snapped his mistress with a smile, and led her guests towards the rear.

They stopped on the top of the gentle rise; turning to face Ingolf's own forces, they had a clear view of most of the field. To one side ran the thick, hoary hedge that had marked the edges of the estate for who knew how long; to the other the meadow sloped gently downwards towards the edge of the river. Behind were trees, gnarled and ancient oaks, birch and beech that stood over the road from the homefield, and then ran southwards to form a little woodland between Eyvindstoft and Hrafnkelsby; beyond where Ingolf and Onund stood with their men, the land stretched out into the beginnings of the long, flat plain that characterised this corner of Mercia, and reached all the way to the hills at its eastern edge. Somewhere behind those intruders, Var realised, there ought to be a marker-stone, the legal end of Thordis' lands; even if Onund had come directly from his own farm, Ingolf must surely have marched his troops over it. She smiled grimly; he *knew* that he was wrong! And yet there he stood, Onund at his side, making ready to come charging towards them with spear and sword and axe...

"Here they come," murmured Asa. "Gods, help us now..."

The noise from their own followers was far louder: in a hoarse, roaring voice, Anlaf put himself at the centre of the line and yelled, "Forwards!" There was no semblance of tactics or good order to it: the whole of the line just hurled itself down the slope towards the incomers in a maelstrom of dust, iron and volume. Var risked a look back: the hidden third had not moved. Then she found her eyes compelled to follow the fight again.

The two forces met with a sound like a house being blown down in a storm, a great, echoing crash of noise as shields splintered, spears drove forward and blades swung wildly. From the watcher's viewpoint, things then settled into a writhing knot of men, not moving around very much but still filled with motion and a strange, violent force all of its own. It went on thus for what seemed like an age: men would move out of the fight, catch their breath and plunge back in; broken weapons would be hurled out of the action to lie unnoticed on the ground. But the fighters never moved far: the mass of men might surge a little one way, then back the other; what had begun as two long, thin lines of warriors was now just a compacted, solid mass of them, all jabbing, battering and slashing at each other, with cries of anger, rage, determination and pain all mingling together in a single song of battle.

"Ingolf's lads are good," commented Thordis almost idly, her eyes fixed on the scene. "Our boys are making no headway against 'em."

"Good thing we held some back, then," said Asa, her own face etched with lines of worry and tiredness. "Want to put 'em in yet?"

"I kept Ingolf talking for as long as I could," came the reply, "but we've still not heard from our little group of spies. I don't want to put in more than we need to without knowing what else *they've* got hidden."

"If we don't," observed Var, "we might be here all day, watching our lads slowly fall before them. It might be that we need to push them back, open up their lines... I'm betting they'll be better equipped than any of ours. It didn't surprise me to see mailshirts on a good few of them; Ingolf's nearly got himself a shipsworth there already."

A number of men had broken away; they ran diagonally across the meadow, heading for... where? From the far line, others fell out of the fight, but not to run, or to rest: there was a new, sudden sound in the air, and the women watched, suddenly horrified, as a thin dark cloud arched across the sky into the runaways. Some fell: a handful did not get up again.

"That was... unexpected..." said Var shakily.

"Don't lose your nerve now," answered Thordis in a harsh voice. "There's worse yet to come if I'm any judge."

"Were it not for the facts of our already having pledged our support, and that your own household is down there dying for your lands as well as ours, I'd be all for giving it up right now," said Asa. Thordis shook her head.

"If we back down now, Onund will be riding to Lisceardr with Var in order to have her daughter to wife; and then he'll be picking off bits of Walea to take for his own." She turned in the saddle to face Asa directly. "If that happens, sister, do you really think he'll ride past Brynjolfsburgh and not stop in to look around?"

"No, of course he wouldn't," Asa spat. "And despite my words, I'm not about to turn tail and let a new power into these lands unchallenged. Nasty little snot that he is," she added scornfully. "More to the point, who were those men that ran?"

"That," said Var, "is something we won't find out until this is over." She edged closer to Thordis. "If you really want this finished once and for all, before all our men are dead or injured, then send in the rest! We're getting nowhere here."

"Who leads them?" asked Thordis. "Anlaf went forward with the main force... I just hope he's still standing. He and Einar have been together in life for so long..."

Var wheeled her horse and trotted what she hoped was an innocent distance. "My man Sigurd's there," she eventually reported. "He's proved himself at Lisceardr over the years."

"Send them down, then, sister, and let's just hope Ingolf hasn't outsmarted us all."

Sigurd took his troops through the trees and hedgerow for as far as he could; suddenly, his men burst out from the summer greenery and smashed into the side of Onund's smaller force. There was an immediate effect: men fell, and the sounds of the fight changed from deep, hoarse roars to an overtone of higher-pitched desperation. To the watching women, it looked as if the single, flowing entity that the battle had become, slowly turned away from the edges of the meadow, then looked for somewhere to retreat to. Horns sounded over the din; men began to break away, leaving the defenders of Eyvindstoft holding their ground, spears levelled, shields to the fore still, awaiting the next charge. The air around them somehow stiffened in their tension; the mood of expectation spread rapidly to the waiting women, who strained forward in their saddles and strove to catch even the faintest idea of what was afoot.

"Do we have to go down there for our news?" grated Thordis impatiently. "If nobody heads our way soon, I'll do it: I swear I will."

"Hush," advised Var, keeping her own eyes just as fixed on the men somehow poised in sudden inactivity. "Neither Anlaf nor Sigurd will keep us waiting any longer than they have to. Look," she exclaimed, gripping Thordis by the arm, "that's Ingolf coming forwards again."

"And he hasn't put any more men in to balance our extras," added Asa. "This could be the talk that sets the rules for his departure."

"Then we ought to be there," urged Thordis. "These boys have just fought a good scrap for us – me – and the least I can do is be there to speak when there's need to."

"And that looks like a runner heading our way," commented Var. "Come then, sister: let's hear the news."

CHAPTER FIFTY-TWO

"Lady," began Ingolf in a breathless but somehow exultant voice under his iron wargear, "you keep strong, fine fighters on your farmstead!" He eventually managed to pull off his helmet and the padded cap beneath it; a shower of sweat sprayed out around him. "You are, I'm sure, proud of every last man of 'em: were they mine, I would be. Treat them well, lady, and I'm sure there will be no further trouble from any quarter whatsoever!"

Thordis inclined her head in thanks. "Can I take it then, sir, that you are withdrawing from these lands of mine?"

"I think we've had enough love-taps for one day," the lord confirmed. "Onund has taken what's left of his men home already: I'm sad to say that he didn't have the stomach for the fight when it finally came down to it. I'm left wondering how much else he had such high words about will turn out to be little more than that."

"I might be able to arrange a meeting with the lady Elfgyfu, his wife," suggested Thordis. Ingolf raised an eyebrow, but said nothing, saving his energy for the alehorn brought over by one of his own men. As he downed it, Thordis looked around.

"I can offer a place for your wounded to be attended to alongside my own, if you would accept it," she said eventually.

"That is generous, and I thank you for it: but home is not so far away for us either, and I don't think any of mine took more than a few well-placed knocks. Your headmen showed good leadership today: they held their men together properly, and never once let fear get hold." He grinned. "A fine fight: but let's hope there is never the need for another one, eh?"

"I suspect, lord, that such things might depend more on Onund than on you or I."

Ingolf snorted derisively. "He'll get no more help from me! I'm not so short of friends that I'd take the trouble to seek out a man who turned and ran at the first clash of spears."

Thordis' eyes widened in shock. "He didn't..."

Ingolf gave her a humourous, appraising stare. "He did! Those men you might have watched running out of the fight earlier were his. I sent the order to shoot 'em down: I won't have that sort of behaviour in my ranks. And that seemed to do for Onund; when I turned back to him, he was gone."

"Well, if he never moves out of Hrafnkelsby again I'll be happy enough," replied Thordis. "Lord, can we leave your men to take themselves back homewards with you? Should I send ale and bread out for them? I have no idea how prepared you were able to be for this..."

Now there was a full laugh from the lord. "My lady, you are kinder by far than you need to be! Rather than provide any further provocation to your own lads, we will depart swiftly. You have my word that my support for Onund in this matter is ended: if he chooses to pursue it even after this, he stands alone as far as I'm concerned. But," he held up a gloved finger, "I must impress on you that your victory here in this affair cannot be taken as any sort of leverage over my or my brother's lordship of these lands. Lady, I must ask for your oath on that; then I can give you mine regarding a distancing from Onund in return."

"I can give that gladly," replied Thordis, "since I never thought to put any greater weight to these events than a dispute over a patch of land! We are all as loyal and true as we always were, my lord: you have my oath to that effect."

"And mine," echoed Var and Asa in turn.

"Then I am glad to give my own oath that I will not come against you in support of Onund after this." He nodded amiably, then turned and ambled back towards his own knot of followers, and the road that led back home.

CHAPTER FIFTY-THREE

"We saw a reflection of our own lords today," mused Var as they sat around the hearth that night. There had not been time to prepare a fitting feast after the events of the day; that would happen tomorrow, when the men had rested and wounds had been seen to. Thordis was adamant that she would wash each and every cut, and bind as many as needed it; but she also reckoned that she would have enough time left in the day to garland the hall and oversee the victory celebrations. Their hastily-assembled men had done well: there were few enough injuries, so fiercely had they carried the fight forward.

Asa dropped out of her own reverie to ponder her neighbour's words. "You think that's what they spend their summers doing, then? And which side of our little scrap did you think resembled them more closely?"

"I know what I want to believe," smiled Var easily. "I want to think that our ship-men looked more like Ingolf's troop than like our gangs, but that they carry their own fights with the same sort of power as our households did today. Then they'd be invincible, against all but the most powerful of opponents."

Asa snorted a laugh. "It was only last year that your Hrolf lost a finger, if you recall! It's things like that which keep me worrying all the time they're away. It makes them men, and not gods in mailshirts... and men can still be hurt, even through their armour. Look at those couple who were carried away today."

For all that she waved a hand dismissilvely, Var's face failed to match her carefree gesture. "They were unlucky," she said, also far from convincingly. "One of them just slipped in a mudpatch and got trampled in the movement; the other caught an axe on the helm and went down from the blow: but he's upright, or was when last I had a glimpse of him, even if he was staggering a bit. But I'll admit we were lucky: we could've had deaths among our boys, and all too easily given their lack of such things as mailshirts and decent helms. As it is, some of the shields'll be good only for the fire; I need to ask Thordis about having her smith take the iron bits off and then she can burn the boards with my blessing." She looked over at her companion suddenly. "Have you taken a tally of your lads yet?"

Now it was Asa's turn to wave a hand carelessly. "It can wait until tomorrow. I reckon everyone's earned a bit of rest."

"Maybe..."

Asa looked across the table at her. "What's nagging you?"

"Onund."

"That little shit? I doubt if we'll see him again! Not only did he turn tail at the first chance, but he had to show up in borrowed gear as well! And then his men deserted him... and now he's lost his only decent ally, too. No, sister, I can't see that there's any need to bother about Onund at all."

"That's because he's not been in your house and sniffing around your children."

"You think he might try something while you're gone from Walea? He'd have to get there first; and then he'd have to get past all the folk you left behind, and say what you might about some of them, they're loyal, and they're true. They'd not let anyone just come in and take the bairns – or the land, or the silver, or much of anything else! Remember, if he was foolish enough to go there, Onund would be travelling on his own: he's not a fine gentleman in good company this time. He's beaten, and tired, and having to fall back on his own wits to see him through; and from what you and Oslac have said, they'll not see him very far at all. No, I reckon he's more likely to hole up in Hrafnkelsby and lick his wounds. If he does that, then he can delude himself that things didn't turn out as badly as was actually the case: that Ingolf betrayed him, that his own bondar proved unequal to the task, and that he stood proudly in the weapon-clash and held his ground, firm in his convictions... and that a gang of impolite, churlish women tricked him out of what ought to be his! Far more in his style, wouldn't you say?"

Var sighed. "You ought to take up with Oslac, you argue a point so well. You're right of course; I just hope I can keep my own worries out of my head well enough to sit at this feasting tomorrow and actually enjoy some of it."

"If it makes you feel any better," offered Asa, "once it's done I could come home with you, just until you're convinced that everything in Lisceardr is still as it should be. We'll have some fine tales for the telling, and no mistake."

"Aye, that we will. I don't expect Thordis will want to go away from here, for exactly the same reasons that I want to bolt for home straight away; but it would be good to guest you for a few nights. Nia can come and swap stories with Hild and Ymma."

"Well that's settled and agreed, then," smiled Asa knowingly. "Now drink your ale and get some of those knots out of your shoulders."

CHAPTER FIFTY-FOUR

"One thing I will say now, that I wouldn't before," confided Asa as she and Var made a leisurely progress homewards a day or two later. "Our new ship-sister strikes me as one to be watched over. Either that or kept at a distance: I just can't decide which."

"I never thought to ask directly, but my guess would be that she's younger than either of us. Maybe it's just that she's not had the experience of holding her ground without resorting to threats and weapons quite so readily," replied Var. "And yet, you know, I'm not so sure that there were many other courses open to her; this was a strange summer, and no mistake. Surely I'm not the only one who's wondering why, if Onund wanted a share in Eyvindstoft so badly, why he never tried to take it when its old master was away on the ship every year."

"Ah, that's easy: the thought of Eyvind coming home and taking it back again would be enough to put even our men off the idea! Imagine Onund sitting in his hall worrying over the consequences: Eyvind would've hit him with everything he had, and even if Hrafnkelsby's master didn't care about his own safety, I bet he'd worry about his mother's. But you heard how he spoke to us even in front of Ingolf: women are nothing to him, so he probably thought he could just march in and take what he wanted without any fear of retribution." She sniffed disdainfully. "Even if it had gone to the Thing eventually, I'm betting he'd've wormed his way out of trouble with fine words and his clean breeks on show."

Var laughed gently. "So our little valkyrie won't have done him any good at all, then! If I could persuade Elle to speak to him in the same fashion, I'm sure he'd rapidly lose any interest there might be remaining in her."

Asa looked over at her companion. "You still worrying about that?"

"I'm sorry: I can't help it. I won't be really settled until I'm back in my own hall and can see that nothing is changed."

Now it was Asa's turn to laugh. "I'd put silver on your not managing it even then!" She looked behind them at the long column of men following. "If you'd give me a few lads to provide an escort back to my own home afterwards," she said, "we could go there directly. I can tell Harald to take my boys back to the burgh, and we could go onwards with just your own folk. You'd be there almost a day sooner."

"I must look like such a fool: I certainly feel like one."

Asa shook her head. "Not at all: you've got enough in Lisceardr to keep you worried, and the bairns would be the least of it. And whilst I don't really think Onund would be mad enough to try anything in the form of vengeance against us, until we know for sure, then it's bound to nag at you."

"Not at you?"

Asa shrugged. "I've less to lose. Oh, he could burn the place down I suppose, but my girl's old enough to handle the household and the boys are away with their uncles. And in some ways, it might be easier to explain a burned house to Brynjolf and get something done about it, than trying to make him accept vague worries and what-ifs."

Var smiled. "And if he were to burn Brynjolfsburgh, well, you know you'd find a welcome in Walea... and at Eyvindstoft too, after all this."

Asa barked another short laugh. "After a summer of intrigue and maneuoverings, a winter in her hall might drive me even madder! Every time she looked towards a bow or an axe, I think I'd flinch at what might be coming next! What if she decided to go wearing breeks or uncovering her arms in company?"

Var's own laugh was louder and longer, and much less forced. "Stop it! You're impossible! I'm sure Thordis would be an impeccable lady of the hall in front of any visitors – even Onund, were he that stupid to think he could get away with such behaviour."

"Hard to imagine what there could be there for him, I'll give you that."

"True: but I bet we'd hear about it just as soon as was able."

CHAPTER FIFTY-FIVE

The long roofline of Lisceardr slowly came into view as they made a weary way through the outfields. Asa's contingent of farmhands had already departed, taking the short road up to the gates of Brynjolfsburgh as they tramped westwards. Perched uncomfortably atop a borrowed pony, Nia had also regarded it rather longingly, before her dark, depth-filled eyes turned again to follow her mistress's back with a long and heavy sigh.

Asa raised an eyebrow. "Don't worry," she said unconcernedly, "we'll be back in a day or two. There's nothing at home so important that it needs you there straight away, surely?" She turned back to Var, without waiting to see if there was an answer.

The road ended at the shores of the river down which the ship had made its own way only a few short moons ago. Walea lay beyond it, almost an island, the only connecting point being the start of the road to Thorsteinn's tun and then onwards to the Mercians. This was one of the places where Ulfketil kept a little flat-bottomed boat, to make a living out of ferrying folk over; but this time, there would be too many for that. The boatman's own face said as much. Asa looked at Var enquiringly.

"We march along the bank," she shrugged in reply. "It's a bit of a longer journey, but not really so far." She looked around at her expectant following. "I need somebody to ride ahead and tell Hild and Ymma that we're nearly home," she called out. "Ulfketil, I'll need to borrow a horse for this: I'll get it back to you tomorrow."

"We have a couple at the house, lady," said the dark-haired ferryman, "and a horse and messenger are easy to ferry across.". Var pointed at a lad standing just behind Sigurd and indicated that he should go with Ulfketil.

"Then we can take our time about it and still have

things ready for us," smiled Var. "You were right, sister: I just needed to be heading home again for my mood to improve."

By the time they reached the river's end, they were skirting the edges of Karlsthorpe and the sun was approaching the waters of the ocean ahead of them. The men let out a quiet cheer as they saw the deserted noust on the far bank; the pace picked up again ever so slightly, as if they were racing the daylight into darkness. But Var held them in line, made them stay on the firm ground of the track, before turning onto the wider road as it came from the southern parts of Wirhalh to meet them.

"The ground around these parts is wet and marshy," she explained to Asa, "and the light's going already. The last thing we need is to start losing folk in the mire, not this close to home."

The lady of Brynjolfsburgh nodded wisely. "Now is the time when they get careless," she agreed. Then she laughed. "It's a good thing they've got us with them, ain't it?"

Perhaps for the first time with this intensity, Var found herself being really glad that her husband had insisted on making a good path from the boatshed up to his hall. It didn't see a lot of use – at least, not on its lower stretches – but it was about to save her the inconvenience of travelling further along the ocean's strand and then through the clustered huts of her bondsmen at the bottom of the slope. She recalled suddenly that she had done nothing about moving anyone into the house formerly held by Solmund and Linden: that would need attending to swiftly, before anyone saw fit to take it on their own. There'd been quite enough of that kind of thinking already this summer, she was sure. And no doubt Thurbrand would be along to grumble at her within a day or so, and Yngvar would be skulking in the dark, warm places where he thought nobody would bother to look for him... and the loom would be calling to her, and she would have to go through the storeroom to see what Hild and Ymma had used up whilst she was away...

And so, with every step into familiar territory, the woman who had adventured as far as Eyvindstoft, had faced down odious suitors and the politest of nobility, and had joined forces with valkyries and lawspeakers, settled back into her true self. *This* was her own kingdom; in these lands, it was her word that ruled, not some other whose motives had to be guessed at, and whose own wants and intentions had sometimes to come above her own. Here, her word was law; here, men ran to do her bidding. And she balanced the needs of house, farm and children effortlessly; it was, after all, what she had been born to.

"Come, sister," she said brightly, with triumph in her voice, "we are nearly there. Be welcome in Lisceardr: let's go up and see what Hild has ready to feast us with."

GLOSSARY

Ath Cliath: a name for the original settlement that later relocated and grew into modern Dublin.

Bere: a primitive six-eared barley introduced by the Vikings.

Bondsman/ Bondar: freemen attached to a social superior, usually in return for support or wages.

Boss: the iron cone or dome at the centre of a shield that protects the hand holding it.

Breeks/ Breeches: knee- length male legwear, often but not always tight- fitting.

Burgh: an Anglo- Saxon term originating in Wessex (see below), denoting a walled or fortified settlement.

Cottar: a lesser rank among the Anglo-Saxon peasantry.

Day- Meal: the Norse generally ate only two meals in a day. Day- Meal was taken around mid- morning, whereas Night- Meal was eaten at or just after sunset.

Dubhllyn: modern Dublin, Ireland.

Felag: a term meaning "fellowship" or "brotherhood", in the sense of a collection of individuals bound together by a common factor or purpose.

Frankland/ Frankia: modern France.

Fyrd: a term denoting a non- professional, seasonal, or conscripted body of fighting- men.

Galweg: modern Galloway in southern Scotland. Another region occupied by Norse exiles from Dublin after the Irish resurgence of 902 AD.

Geld/ Wergeld: payment made in compensation for killings or woundings.

Hauldr/ Hauldar: a position within Norse society. Lower to middle aristocracy: literally, a holder of land.

Heddle: the horizontal bar on a loom, used to hold separate groups of threads apart.

Herred: the Norse equivalent of the English Hundred (see Wapentak).
Hird: a term denoting a professional or semiprofessional body of fighting men (see Fyrd above).
Hooded One: a name used of Odin, the God of death and wisdom.
Howe: a burial mound.
Jarl: a position within Norse society, equivalent to an English Eorl or Earl.
Karlsthorpe: modern Bidston, Wirral.
Kyrtle: an overshirt or outer tunic.
Lady's Bedstraw: a herb used in straw mattresses to control animal infestation.
Lawman/ Lawspeaker: an official whose function was to memorise, recite and enforce the local law codes.
Legacaester: modern Chester.
Lisceardr: modern Liscard, on the Wirral.
Longphort: the original fortified ship-bases of the Norse in Ireland. Many modern Irish cities are descended from them, especially on the eastern coast.
Mann: the modern Isle of Man.
Maserfieth: modern Wigan, in Merseyside.
Meols: a site on Wirral, thought to possibly have been a beach market. Finds from the nineteenth century are currently undergoing re- evaluation, and it may be that Meols was actually a burial site.
Mercia: one of the English kingdoms, covering the modern Midlands and North- West England.
Mere: a lake or pool.
North- Way: modern Norway.
Noust: a boat shed.
Odal: term denoting the hereditary or customary ownership of land.
Ongle-sey: modern Angelsey in North Wales.
Oslofjord: southern Norway, at this time still a separate kingdom. Site of the Tune, Oseberg and Gokstad ship- burials.

Portage: the practice of hauling a ship overland between waterways.
Pottage: a barley-based stew with herbs.
Rake: a name for a narrow lane or sheep-track, used locally on the Wirral.
Rangerike: south-western Norway, at this time a recently-absorbed separate kingdom.
Sogn: another recently-absorbed Norwegian petty kingdom.
Saga: a traditional form of Norse story-telling, analagous to a modern historical novel.
Se'en-night: literally seven nights, ie, a week.
Skald: a poet; often also genealogist, propagandist and keeper of other useful information.
Skive: term denoting the shaving-off of a portion of something, usually used in relation to leatherworking.
Snickleway: a narrow alley off a wider street.
Stofa: the main living-room of a longhouse, where the central hearth was.
Strathclyde: modern South West Scotland.
Tafl: a generic term for a number of similar boardgames. Also known as Hnaefatafl, or King's Table.
Thing: a meeting of free-born men, of all social strata, for the purposes of law-making and legal disputation. Roughly analagous to a combined District Council and Magistrate's Court, and often including trade fairs and social gatherings.
Thorsteinnstun: modern Thurstaston, in Wirral.
Thrall: a slave, although this was not necessarily a life-long or immutable state.
Tun: in English, a village, but in Norse, a farmstead. One of a number of interchangeable terms.
Valkyrie: supernatural "choosers of the slain": handmaidens of Odin in his role as leader of an army of heroic dead.
Vestfold: modern South West Norway.
Vik: modern southern Norway, the area of modern Oslofjord.

Walea: modern Wallasey, on Wirral, Merseyside.
Wall-plates: long horizontal beams placed along the tops of wooden or wattle walls; part of the houseframe which took the weight of the roof down to the ground.
Wapentak Court: the Norse equivalent of the English Hundred: an administrative unit of land, roughtly analagous to a modern county. Each Wapentak had its own court which settled internal disputes.
Weld: a dye-giving plant, usually producing a bright range of yellow hues.
Weregeld: a payment, usually compensation for blood-letting or killings, made by the perpetrator of the crime in order to avoid either outlawry or revenge-killings.
Wessex: one of the English Kingdoms, covering South West England.
Westmorland: modern Cumbria and Strathclyde.
Wherington: modern Warrington, Cheshire.
Wirhalh: modern Wirral, Merseyside.
Wyrd: usually interpreted as "fate", but in its original context, wyrd is more flexible and subject to change at every moment.

Printed in Great Britain
by Amazon